"It's time to e[r]
get in any de[___]

Jarett took a coup[le of] steps toward her. "Are you talking about the body-double scheme we pulled off? Or something else?"

Meg twisted the towel she was holding and looked at him from lowered lashes. "What else would I be talking about?" she asked.

Jarett's jeans became uncomfortably tight. He knew he should keep things strictly business between them, but he couldn't. He wanted her—more than he'd ever wanted anything. He wanted her hair falling down around him and her glasses steamed up. He wanted to give them both a night to remember before they returned to the real world.

He crossed the room in a few quick strides, and curving his hand around the nape of her neck, he pulled her up to meet his hard, hungry kiss. He slid his hands up her back and into her hair, causing the silky tresses to slip out of their confines and fall down her back.

His body leapt in anticipation and raw desire. Taking a step back, he looked into her bright green eyes. "But Meg, this could be just the beginning...."

Blaze™

Dear Reader,

This month marks the launch of a supersexy new series—
Harlequin Blaze. If you like love stories with a strong sexual
edge, then this is the line for you! The books are fun and
flirtatious, the heroes are hot and outrageous. Blaze is a
series for the woman who wants *more* in her reading
pleasure....

Leading off the launch is bestselling author
Vicki Lewis Thompson, who brings us a heroine to
remember in the aptly titled #1 *Notorious*. Then popular
Jo Leigh delivers a blazing story in #2 *Going for It*, about
a sex therapist who ought to take her own advice. One of
today's hottest writers, Stephanie Bond, spins a humorous
tale of sexual adventure in #3 *Two Sexy!* Rounding out
the month is talented Julie Elizabeth Leto with the romp
#4 *Exposed*, which exposes the sexy side of San Francisco
and is the first of the SEXY CITY NIGHTS miniseries.

Look for four Blaze books every month at your favorite
bookstore. And check us out online at eHarlequin.com
and tryblaze.com.

Enjoy!

Birgit Davis-Todd
Senior Editor & Editorial Coordinator
Harlequin Blaze

TWO SEXY!
Stephanie Bond

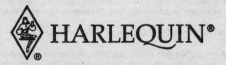

HARLEQUIN®

TORONTO • NEW YORK • LONDON
AMSTERDAM • PARIS • SYDNEY • HAMBURG
STOCKHOLM • ATHENS • TOKYO • MILAN • MADRID
PRAGUE • WARSAW • BUDAPEST • AUCKLAND

This book is dedicated to the folks behind the scenes
at Harlequin, who work to bring us romantic
entertainment month after month:
the editorial department, the art department, the production
department, the sales department, the marketing department,
the public relations department and eHarlequin.
Thank you, thank you, thank you.

ISBN 0-373-79007-4

TWO SEXY!

Copyright © 2001 by Stephanie Bond Hauck.

Visit us at www.eHarlequin.com

Printed in U.S.A.

A NOTE FROM THE AUTHOR...

Welcome to Blaze! I'm thrilled to be a part of this exciting new line and even more excited by the possibilities now open to us—as authors and readers.

If you missed *Midnight Fantasies*, the July 2001 Blaze collection, you missed meeting Rebecca Valentine, owner of Anytime Costumes. But you're about to meet her sister, Meg, who agrees to run the shop while Rebecca is on her honeymoon. Meg Valentine is a teacher who's yearning for a little excitement before accepting a proposal from her longtime boyfriend. Taking the job as a body double for a celebrity sex kitten certainly fits the bill! And while wearing provocative clothing and evading the paparazzi are eye-opening experiences, Meg soon discovers the most risqué part of her employment is working closely, *very* closely, with seriously sexy Jarett Miller. Get ready for the sparks to fly!

If you've been waiting for a longer, more sensual read, the wait is over.... Blaze has arrived! Don't forget to share the good news with a friend—she'll thank you.

For a complete list of my titles, visit my Web site at www.stephaniebond.com.

Stephanie Bond

1

"AMAZING. LISTEN TO THIS."

Meg Valentine looked over the top of her BLT sandwich at her best friend, Kathie, sprawled in a chair in the teachers' lounge.

"The wedding of actors Elyssa Adams and John Bingham cost a reported one million dollars. The gown alone set the couple back fifty thousand, and the cake, twenty thousand." Kathie lowered the magazine. "Twenty thousand bucks for a lousy cake, and it probably wasn't even chocolate. Do you realize that's how much money I'll *net* this year?"

Meg grinned, chewing. Besides being a chronic complainer, Kathie was a Hollywood aficionado—the woman spent every disposable dollar on celebrity memorabilia—props from movie sets, scripts, even a lock or two of hair from famous people. And she lived for every outrageous headline the tabloids could deliver.

"Those people live in a different world," Sharon, another teacher, offered, pointing her fork at Kathie. "And I'll bet it's not nearly as rosy as you think."

"Right," piped in Joanna from the corner, who spent her lunch hours knitting scarves for Christmas gifts. "Those people have problems, just like the rest of us."

"But they lead such exciting lives." A faraway expression came over Kathie's face. "Wearing gorgeous clothes, having men fall at your feet. Wouldn't it be grand to live in a celebrity's shoes for just a few days?"

Meg shook her head. "Kathie, you're such a dreamer."

"Yeah," Sharon said. "Face it—we're elementary school teachers in Peoria, Illinois. We gave up 'exciting' when we made our career choice." The women laughed.

Except for Meg, who bit into a pickle, digesting the bittersweet truth of Sharon's words. She truly loved teaching and working with children, but sometime during the last few years, her life *had* fallen into a serious rut when she wasn't looking. Cabin fever, hormones, early-life crisis—she couldn't explain her sudden restlessness. All she knew was that lately she was easily distracted from her evening routine of grading math papers, and ready to come out of her very proper skin. Perhaps she'd sensed Trey's impending proposal, something she still wasn't sure she knew how to handle.

Kathie scooted to the edge of her seat, her hazel eyes dancing. "This weekend I'm going to Indy for a fan festival. They're supposed to auction off some wardrobe items from the set of *Many Moons.*"

Kathie's favorite show. She'd even managed to get the three of them hooked on the weekly melodrama. Every Wednesday night they congregated at Kathie's apartment and munched popcorn while watching the beautiful people make multi-million dollar deals, stab each other in the back, and steal each other's lovers. Most of the scenes took place near or on the beach, which meant the costumes were one of two types—scanty or nonexistent.

Sharon scoffed. "What will you do with clothes from *Many Moons?* Wear them to the PTA potluck?"

They all laughed again, but Kathie shook her finger. "You just wait, my collection is going to be worth something someday."

She turned to another page in the magazine that featured The Sexiest Outfits of the Season. Kathie pointed to a picture of Taylor Gee, the actress who played the curvaceous blonde vixen on *Many Moons,* wearing a transparent yellow gown. "This dress is my next conquest."

"Is she wearing underwear?" Joanna asked, the knitting forgotten as she craned her head in for a look.

Meg pushed up her glasses and squinted at the telltale dark areas beneath the dress, stretched to the limit of its seams by the actress's remarkable curves. "I don't think so."

"Ewww," Sharon said. "You want to buy a dress she wore with no underwear?"

Kathie made a face. "I'll have it drycleaned, idget. The point is, it's going to be a collector's item."

"What makes you think so?" Meg asked.

"Taylor Gee is the closest thing to Marilyn Monroe this generation has ever known. And similarly, from the glazed look on her face, she's going to burn up before she burns out."

They all leaned in for a better look, but Meg saw only an impossibly beautiful woman in an impossibly scanty gown. Her head was turned and she was smiling at someone—the man who was cropped out of the photo? Only the sleeve of his black jacket remained, emblazoned with some kind of crest. Probably someone famous. The woman had been linked with every international bad boy there was, from rock star to rebel prince.

"I can't believe she would go out in public wearing something like that," Sharon said, shaking her head. "She's already gorgeous. Why does she need to be so over the top?"

"So she'll make the Sexiest Outfits of the Season list," Meg pointed out.

"And so pathetic people like us will spend our lunch hour talking about her," Joanna chimed in.

"Deep down, we all wish we could wear a dress like that," Kathie insisted, tapping the page. "And turn every person's head when we walk into a room."

At times Kathie sounded more like a psychology teacher than a science teacher. She had a knack for zeroing in on people's deepest, darkest urges. Meg had picked up the phone a couple times this week to talk to her friend about her general state of unrest, but she'd changed her mind at the last second. She couldn't seem to zero in on what was wrong with her. Spring fever? Cold feet?

"Even if that was true," Joanna said, flipping her head of carrot-orange curls, "we don't all look like Taylor Gee."

"Meg is beautiful enough to pull it off," Sharon insisted, and to Meg's chagrin, all eyes turned to her. Her neck and cheeks warmed, and she pushed her glasses higher on her nose. "Don't be ridiculous."

"Take off your glasses," Kathie urged.

"What? No."

"Come on, humor me."

Meg slipped off her glasses and sighed.

"I can't believe I never noticed."

"What, the hump on my nose?"

"No—you're a dead ringer for Taylor Gee."

Meg squinted in Kathie's direction. "Maybe *you* should borrow my glasses."

"Am I right, girls?"

Sharon hummed. "Well, if your hair was blond—"

"—and if your eyes were blue," Joanna chimed in.

"—and if you painted a mole near the corner of your mouth," Sharon continued.

"—and if you were coming out of your clothes," Joanna offered, "then yeah, you'd be a dead ringer for her."

"See?" Kathie asked.

Meg laughed and jammed the black rimmed glasses back on her face. "You three watch too much TV."

Kathie grinned. "You have the face, but those baggy dresses would not get you on the Sexiest Outfits of the Season list."

Meg frowned and looked down at her gray crinkle cotton dress. "I like my baggy dresses.

They're comfortable. And washable." An important feature when working with seven-year-olds.

"Meg probably wears something more sexy for Trey," Joanna teased.

She squirmed. In truth, Trey Carnegie liked the fact that she didn't flaunt her body. *You dress like a lady—you always make me proud to stand next to you.* Too bad Meg wasn't sure she wanted Trey to always treat her like a "lady." She cleared her throat. "Speaking of Trey, I have an announcement."

The room fell silent.

"Last night after the benefit dinner...Trey proposed."

Sharon and Joanna squealed their congratulations, and even Kathie managed a little smile.

"Well, Mr. Three Piece Suit finally got around to it, eh?"

There was no love lost between Kathie and Trey, but Meg had stopped trying to figure out why her closest friend didn't gel with her long-time boyfriend. Trey said Kathie was jealous because she didn't have a boyfriend. But Meg couldn't disagree with her friend on one point—Trey had taken his sweet time asking for her hand—five years. And Meg still wasn't sure why she waited.

"What did you tell him?" Kathie asked.

"What do you think she told him?" Sharon asked a little sarcastically.

"I don't see a ring."

Sharon glanced at Meg's bare left hand, then gasped. "What did you tell him?"

Meg looked at the three curious faces, and the familiar weight of expectation settled in her stomach. Meg the good girl. Meg the straight-A student. Meg the model employee. Meg the proper girlfriend. God, she wanted to break free from it all. She inhaled. "I said I needed some time to think about it."

Kathie slapped her knee. "Good for you."

"She's just paying him back for making her wait so long," Joanna said. "Aren't you, Meg?"

She wished. Her mother was practically frantic about her sister Rebecca's broken engagement, then her rebound romance with Michael Pierce that seemed to be moving way too quickly. Once again, the pressure was on Meg to do the right thing. So to be honest, she had no idea why she hadn't told Trey "yes" on the spot, except for the underlying feeling that there was something missing. Like romance. Passion. Excitement. Still, Joanna's explanation seemed good enough for now. "Right. I'm going to let him cool his heels for a while."

"And who knows?" Kathie said with a sly

grin. "In the meantime, maybe you'll meet someone who'll make you forget all about Trey Carnegie."

"Kathie," Joanna chided, "Trey is a catch, especially around here."

That was odd. Did Joanna mean that if they weren't in Peoria, Trey wouldn't be as good a catch? But she knew what her friend meant—young, successful men from prominent wealthy families did not grow on trees in their quaint city.

"Did he offer you a ring?" Sharon asked, a wistful look in her eyes.

"He wants me to pick it out when I'm ready."

"Did you tell him when you'd give him an answer?" Joanna asked, equally starry-eyed.

Guilt twinged low in Meg's stomach—both Joanna and Sharon would change places with her in a split-second, and here she was stalling. "I told him we'd talk about it when I get back from vacation. I'm taking off all next week."

Kathie whooped. "You're finally taking the five-day bonus they gave you for being Teacher of the Year?"

That was a source of pride *and* embarrassment. In fact, maybe some of the disquiet she'd been experiencing could be posttraumatic stress over the wave of statewide publicity she'd received the past couple of months. More expectations. Meg nodded sheepishly.

"Well, it's about time."

"Where are you going?" Sharon asked.

"Somewhere exciting?" Joanna asked.

"A cruise?"

"The beach?"

"Vegas?"

Meg folded her napkin and patted her mouth. "I'm going to Chicago to run my sister's costume shop."

In the ensuing silence, she got the feeling her friends were a little underwhelmed.

"Oh."

"That's nice."

"Er, yes, very nice."

Meg sipped on her straw. The end of her fountain soda greeted her with a great sucking noise.

"That doesn't sound like much of a vacation," Kathie said finally.

"No, it doesn't," Sharon agreed.

"Not at all," Joanna said.

"No, but I'm glad to do it," Meg said. In fact, she'd been counting the days. She needed a change of scenery, time to think. "It'll be fun. And Rebecca needs me."

"Really, Meg," Kathie said dryly. "One of

these days you're going to have to live a more sedate life.''

Meg stuck out her tongue and the girls laughed. Then the bell rang. They groaned and gathered the remnants of their lunch.

''Do you ever have the feeling that your life revolves around bells?'' Meg asked.

Kathie frowned. ''I hear that darn thing in my sleep.''

Meg sighed as they walked out into the clattering hall, once again gripped by a quiet fear she couldn't put her finger on. Miles of battered lockers, acres of scuffed floors, the din of hundreds of little voices, the lingering odor of paper and paste. Was this really where she belonged?

''Depressing, isn't it?'' Kathie asked, taking in the same scene.

''No,'' Meg said too quickly. ''I love my job.''

''I love my job, too,'' Kathie said with a wry smile. ''But I can't say that I love the fact that all the men in my life are Cub Scouts.''

''You could date if you wanted to,'' Meg said. ''What about your neighbor, the doctor?''

''Oh, right—I've seen the man twice. The first time he said hello, I closed my hand in the car door. The second time, I walked into the mailbox. I think I've burned my bridges where he's concerned—even a doctor doesn't have that much insurance.'' She sighed dramatically. "No, I've re-signed myself to spinsterhood.''

"We're only twenty-seven, Kathie. We won't be spinsters for at least another three years.'' *Three short years...*

She smirked. "So what's the real reason you didn't say yes to Trey? Having second thoughts?''

"No, I told you—''

"You're making him pay.'' Kathie shook her head. "I don't buy it, Meg. You don't have a vindictive bone in your body.''

Meg sunk her teeth into her bottom lip, surprised at Kathie's sudden gravity.

Then her friend sighed. "Whatever the reason, make sure you take as long as you need to decide whether or not Trey is the man for you.''

At a loss for words, Meg simply nodded.

Then her friend grinned again, and elbowed her in the ribs. "I still can't believe you've got an entire week away from this place, and you're going to spend it *working*.''

"I won't be working the entire time,'' Meg protested. "I'll have my evenings free, and two Sundays.''

Her friend wagged her eyebrows. "Oooh, maybe I should come with you to keep you out of trouble.''

Even Meg had to laugh—she'd never been in

trouble in her life. "Have fun at the fan festival—I hope you find that naughty dress you're looking for."

"Shhhh!" Kathie looked around, then moved in close. "If Principal O'Banion even hears the word 'naughty,' she'll start digging into my personal life."

Meg scoffed. "You're exaggerating."

"Tell that to Amanda Rollins."

"The art teacher? What about her?"

"Well, no one is supposed to know this yet, but she was fired yesterday."

"*What?* Why?"

"Apparently someone saw her renting an X-rated movie at a local video store."

Meg's jaw dropped. "Can they fire her for that?"

"They did. She was 'supposedly' violating the 'moral behavior' code of our employment contract."

"That's a pretty loose interpretation."

Kathie shrugged. "But it's the school board's interpretation to make. Me, I get my X-rated movies through the mail."

Meg blinked.

"I'm kidding," Kathie said.

Meg shook her head. "Poor Amanda. The kids love her."

"That kind of scrutiny comes with the territory. Not that you have anything to worry about, Miss Teacher of the Year." She gave Meg a nudge.

Meg managed a smile despite the tightness in her chest. It was supposed to be a compliment— the honor, the title—but honestly, some days she felt like an Osmond.

Her friend patted her arm. "Hey, if I don't talk to you before you leave, have a great time in Chicago. And if you see anyone famous, get their autograph for me?"

Kathie covered every angle. "Okay, but the only celebrity I've ever met was a distant Kennedy relation at one of Trey's father's fundraisers."

"Keep your eyes open. And try to cut loose a little, okay? Enjoy what may be your last week as an unfettered woman."

Meg wet her lips, but the bell rang again, so she simply manufactured a little smile that matched her expression in those Teacher of the Year posters plastered everywhere. "I'm just looking forward to not hearing a bell ring for an entire week."

And to a few days where nobody knew how perfect she was.

2

"SHE WON'T OPEN THE DOOR," the hairdresser said, his hands jammed on his slim hips. "*Do* something."

Jarett Miller closed his eyes and counted to ten. If only he could open them and be somewhere other than Los Angeles, in the ostentatious home of the most spoiled woman in the world. He opened his eyes, but the irate hairdresser still stood there, his toe tapping.

"I'll see what I can do." Jarett tossed aside the tabloid that featured the latest exploits of his charge, then dragged himself up from the overstuffed, overpriced sofa. His chest filled with dread with each step he took across the great room, through the hall, and up the sweeping stairs—red-carpeted, of course. Nothing less for Taylor Gee, the toast of Tinseltown, sex kitten of the hour.

As his hand slid over the garish gold-tone banister, he marveled at the differences between the lavish home she'd bought for herself and the modest home Taylor Jean Gumm had grown up in in rural West Virginia. "Bought" was a generous term, since she'd mortgaged herself into old age for the monstrosity, against his advice. But then, Taylor didn't take advice well when it meant she couldn't have everything she wanted.

Rosie, Taylor's personal assistant, stood in front of the door to Taylor's suite, hopping from foot to foot. "Please, Miss Gee, unlock the door!"

Rosie was a little round-faced woman who had plenty of nervous energy to do Taylor's bidding. She reminded Jarett of a small dog that had gotten its tail stepped on so many times, it remained in perpetual motion. She moved aside as Jarett approached, visibly shaking. "Oh, good. She's been asking for you."

"Is she high?" he asked.

Rosie sighed. "I don't think so, just depressed."

Jarett bit down on the inside of his cheek. Taylor was beautiful, famous, and rich—from where he was standing, she had little to be depressed about. But what did he know? He was just a country boy, trapped in a town he hated as a result of a promise he'd made.

He rapped on the door sharply. "Taylor, it's Jarett. Open the door."

A few sniffles sounded on the other side. "No."

He swallowed a string of curses. "You're expected at the cast party in an hour."

More sniffles. "I don't want to go."

It was a game she played that Jarett called Beg Me. He opened his mouth to play out the situation, then changed his mind. "Okay, I'll call Peterson and ask him to make your excuses."

He counted to three.

"No, wait," she said, her voice plaintive, but amazingly stronger.

"I'm waiting," he said.

"Are you alone?"

He nodded to Rosie. "Take a break. I'll find you if she needs you."

The woman scampered away, and Jarett pulled his hand down his face, making a mental note to have the door keyed, and to keep a key on his ring. "I'm alone, Taylor." And nearly at the end of his patience.

After a few seconds, he heard the deadbolt turn. When the door didn't open, he turned the knob and entered her suite.

Taylor stood in the pink-and-gold living room near a window, facing him and smoking a long cigarette. Her mane of blond hair was mussed and her mascara smudged. She was wearing high-heeled mules and a short transparent robe. And nothing else. Her limbs were long and lean, her breasts voluptuous and taut. The hair at the juncture of her thighs had been reduced to a tiny triangle to accommodate the scanty swimwear she wore on the set. A cultivated tan covered every square inch of her body. Taylor smiled lazily.

Jarett set his jaw and turned his back. "Put something on."

"Why?" she purred. "Does seeing me like this do things to you, Jarett?"

He'd seen her naked a hundred times—Taylor was an exhibitionist who delighted in shocking people. "It only makes me wonder what's going on in that head of yours."

He heard her muted footsteps on the thick carpet, then she was in front of him, lifting her arms around his neck, pushing her body into his. "You know what's in my head, Jarett. I want you."

Taylor used to be an incredible beauty, but a year of hard partying had taken its toll, and the daylight wasn't kind to her unmade face. Her eyes were slightly glazed, and her lips pouty. She reeked of stale smoke and perspiration. He itched to yank the cigarette out of her hand but considering her other vices, this one was relatively harmless. Sadness welled in his chest at the cliché she had become.

Jarett clasped her wrists gently, and turned her around. "Taylor, stop this childish routine." He shrugged out of his standard black jacket and put it around her slender shoulders. "I wouldn't be here if I didn't care about you, but not in that way."

"You're just afraid David will be mad at you if you sleep with me," she said as she walked away. "But David knows his little sister is all grown up."

Jarett pursed his mouth. "Let's hope that David doesn't get the tabloids at his missionary camp in Haiti. And it's a good thing that your folks don't own a television."

She flounced down on one of the twin pink sofas. "Isn't that a gas? I'm one of the biggest stars on TV, and my own parents have never seen my show." She took a drag from the cigarette. "Really, sometimes I can't believe I came from such a hick family."

Anger sparked low in his stomach. "Don't talk about your family that way. They're good people."

Her laugh was dry as she looked up at him from the couch. "I know—salt of the earth, God-fearing people. And I'm glad they took you in, Jarett, really I am. I just wish you'd stop thinking of me as your little sister. There are thousands, maybe millions of men who'd love to sleep with me, you know."

He refrained from mentioning that a good number of them already had. She opened her knees slightly to give him another glance at what she was offering, but Jarett had developed a rather clinical attitude toward Taylor's nudity. "Put your legs together, and act like a lady."

She scoffed, but complied. "A lady? Is that what you're holding out for, Jarett—a lady? You're in the wrong town, old friend."

Don't I know it. And his lack of female companionship the last year or so had proved it. "I'm only here to look out for you," he said finally, crossing his arms. "Although I don't believe I'm doing such a good job."

She grinned, took another drag, then smashed the cigarette butt into a lead crystal ashtray the size of a dinner plate. "Don't be so hard on yourself, Jarett. You follow me like a goddamned bloodhound, and you keep the freaks at bay."

He walked over to the wet bar and picked up an empty bottle of vodka. "Those freaks don't pose nearly as much of a threat as the things you do to yourself."

"Booze loosens me up," she said with a sigh. "You ought to try it sometime."

He opened a drawer that held drinking glasses

and reached in the back to pull out a handful of prescription bottles. "And what do the pills do?"

She blanched, then recovered with a glib smile. "The pills give me a boost of energy when I need it, that's all."

"You've been needing a boost a lot lately."

She arched an eyebrow. "You *have* been keeping an eye on me."

He set the pills aside, then walked over and eased down on the couch opposite her, hoping that some part of the small-town girl he remembered remained to reason with. "Taylor, I think after the trip to Chicago, you should check yourself into a rehab clinic."

She frowned. "Don't be ridiculous. It's not like I'm an addict or anything."

"Good. Then it should be easy for you to give up the pills and the booze. You're on hiatus from the show, so it'll be a good time to get some rest and to get clean."

"No way—the tabloids will have a field day."

"You haven't seen today's headlines—they're already having a field day. That stunt you pulled at Zago's restaurant the other night has everyone speculating about what you're hooked on."

She scoffed again. "Can't a girl dance on a table without everyone thinking she's on drugs?"

"But you were on drugs."

"Jarett, for heaven's sake, you make it sound like I'm a coke head or something."

"Or something," he said, nodding.

"The doctor *gave* me those pills," she said, her eyes bright.

"Some of the doctors you've been dealing with are little more than drug dealers," he said quietly. "Peterson called this morning, and he said the network is getting concerned about your behavior. He said one more stunt, and your career could be on the line."

"Peterson isn't the only agent in town," she said lightly.

"Taylor, listen to yourself. You jumped through hoops to sign with Peterson's agency— he's one of the best and you know it. He's the reason you got the part on *Many Moons*."

She sat up, scowling. "*I* got myself that part. No one could play Tess Canton the way I do."

He nodded thoughtfully. "You're right. But you're letting the character take over your life. And it's not pretty."

Her face screwed up in anger and she bounced up from the couch, his jacket swinging around her. "Oh, so now you don't even think I'm pretty?" She started crying.

Jarett sighed and held up his hands. "I didn't

say that. Of course you're pretty. You're beautiful, Taylor.''

She managed a smile through her tears. "You think so?''

"Yes," he said levelly. "Now, are you going to the cast party, or are you going to disappoint your fans?''

She inhaled, then sighed prettily. "I'm going to the cast party.''

"Good." He stood up.

"Do you have to go, Jarett?'' Her face crumpled, and his chest squeezed at her desperate tone.

He wished he could help Taylor, but his sympathy didn't extend to having an empty physical relationship with her. He'd promised his best friend, David, that he'd take care of his sister until David returned from Haiti to step in. In addition to the bond they'd forged when David and Taylor's parents had taken him in as a teenager, he and David had joined the Air Force and trained side by side for four years. They were closer than most brothers, and Jarett would gladly have put his life on the line for David. Although some days, he thought the two-year promise he'd made to his friend *would* be the death of him.

"I have to get a car lined up for tonight," he said with the best smile he could muster. "And another guard to help me keep the, um, *freaks* at bay.''

''Okay. Do you want your jacket back?'' she teased.

''I'll get it later,'' he said breezily, backing away before she could take it off and offer it to him.

She sighed. ''What would I do without you, Jarett?''

''You don't have to worry about that,'' he said sincerely, then handily changed the subject. ''Your hairdresser is downstairs ready to have a stroke.''

She drove her hands into her wild, white-blond hair. ''Okay, send him up—tell him I'm jumping in the shower.'' A yawn overtook her and her entire body seemed to deflate with fatigue.

''No pills tonight,'' Jarett said with a pointed look.

''No pills,'' she agreed, although her voice was less than convincing.

He left her suite and found Rosie to let her know that Taylor was back on track for the time being, but as he walked downstairs, Jarett's booted feet were heavy. He had a bad feeling that Taylor was going down the same path many ill-fated starlets had taken before—drugs, alcohol, and ultimate destruction if she didn't get help soon.

He felt guilty as hell that her infatuation with him seemed to be driving her closer to the edge. In reality, he knew Taylor struggled with low self-esteem. She craved approval, especially from her intensely religious family. At times, it seemed as if she behaved so outrageously just to get their attention.

He also suspected that her preoccupation with him was rooted in the fact that she couldn't have him. She knew her family would be scandalized if the two of them became involved. But he wasn't willing to sleep with her just to prove his theory. Instead he held out hope that someday she'd meet a decent guy who would make her feel good about herself. To date, however, all her boy-friends had been first-class losers.

But the worst part of the entire situation was that, at one time, he *had* fancied himself to be in love with Taylor. When he and David had joined the Air Force to travel the world, Taylor had been a gangly girl of twelve. When they returned to Wheeling, West Virginia, she was a voluptuous woman of eighteen. He'd been enchanted by her, and Taylor had made no secret about the fact that she'd waited for him. But the Gumms had trusted him completely, so he'd set aside his feelings and discouraged her advances.

When Taylor announced that after graduation, she was going to L.A. to become an actress, Mr. and Mrs. Gumm were horrified, especially since they'd tried to shelter their daughter from the ways of the world by banning TV and rock and roll music from their household. But when they realized their stubborn little girl was not to be denied, they agreed to let her go, as long as David and Jarett went along to look after her.

From the get-go, Jarett had hated L.A., but he was more worldly than either David or Taylor, so he'd stayed to make sure nobody got into trouble. The three of them had shared an apartment. He and David had gotten work in the security business, and took turns accompanying Taylor to auditions. She'd landed enough modeling shoots and commercials to keep her spirits high. David, on the other hand, was miserable. So when his father had presented him with a two-year missionary opportunity in Haiti, David had happily left Taylor to Jarett's charge.

Nobody knew that Jarett had been miserable, too. Taylor was coming into her own as a woman and tempting him at every turn in the close quarters they shared. At the same time, some of the less pleasant aspects of Taylor's personality were also coming to light—she had a cutting tongue, a dirty mouth, and was prone to outlandish tantrums when she didn't get her way. And when Jarett had made it clear they wouldn't be lovers, she'd retaliated by bringing a string of bozos back to their apartment.

But she'd continued to perform well, and on one of Jarett's security jobs, he'd had the occasion to do a favor for Mac Peterson, a first-class talent agent. The man had agreed to interview Taylor, and had taken her on. When she'd landed the role of Tess Canton on *Many Moons,* Taylor became an overnight sensation. Publicity agent Sheila Waterson came on board to manage Taylor's public appearances, and Jarett had taken over her personal security. Her photo was now one of the most downloaded images on the Internet, and one of her swimsuit posters was the number five bestselling poster of all time.

They had created a monster, it seemed.

Jarett signaled the flustered hairdresser to go on up to Taylor's suite, then walked to the phone to call Peterson. "Taylor's going to the cast party," he assured the man on the line.

"Thank Gawd," Peterson said, his British accent seemingly more pronounced today. "Do you think you can keep her away from the booze?"

"I'll try."

"And everything else?"

"Again, I'll try. But I can't be with her every second."

"Seeing as how I've been on the phone for the last hour covering her tracks for that nasty little table dance she did at Zago's, I think you'd better stay as close as possible. Ditto for the Chicago trip, Jarett. She'll be under the network's microscope. No more see-through frocks."

He sighed. "Fine time for Sheila to be out of town."

"Sheila's managing too many high-maintenance personalities. I'm counting on you to handle Taylor until Sheila returns from Mexico with her kleptomaniac rock star."

"You know I'll do my best."

"Yes, I do, Jarett. Taylor's bloody lucky to have you."

He thanked the man, then hung up. An ache had set up at the base of his skull. He walked to the window of the opulent living room and looked out over the cramped, arid landscape—houses sat on every possible inch of ground, and crisscrossed power lines ruined what might have been a passable view. The only color relieving the sea of red tile roofs were dots of blue—swimming pools. The people in this neighborhood preferred concrete to grass.

It was selfish he knew, but he was practically counting the days until David returned. By then Taylor would be almost twenty-one and he could walk away with a clear conscience. He was tired of fake people and big crowds and loud parties. He planned to find a cabin in some remote part of the country and hole up with a fishing pole for an extended period of time. No TV, no telephone, no women.

Because if he'd learned nothing else the past couple of years with Taylor, he'd learned he was better off alone than to be tangled up with a woman who messed with his head. At times he wondered if he and Taylor had gotten together when he returned from the Air Force, things would've turned out differently. The electricity between them had been palpable in the beginning, and he had to admit, he'd never been so affected by any other woman. But Taylor was Taylor, and everything and everyone in her life paled next to her quest for stardom. He was being arrogant if he thought a relationship between them would have helped matters. If anything, it would have made matters worse. And probably splintered his bond with the entire Gumm family.

It was a shame that Taylor couldn't have been satisfied with the love of one man instead of millions of men. A shame that instead of possessing the generous disposition shared by the rest of her family, that Taylor was like poison to the people who came in contact with her. Love was wasted on her.

Jarett laughed at his preposterous musings. What he dreamed about was a woman who had a face like Taylor Gee, but had a heart of gold—absurd. She didn't exist. And if she did, he didn't want to meet her, because he'd be a lost man.

3

A FEW DAYS LATER Meg descended the stairs
leading from her sister's tiny apartment down to
the workroom of the costume shop. Rebecca's
Murphy bed had been comfortable enough, but
Meg hadn't slept well—too many thoughts spinning in her head, too many decisions to make.
One minute marrying Trey made perfect sense,
the next minute she wondered if marrying him
would be selling out, the path of least resistance.

She flipped on lights as she moved through the
workroom cluttered with sewing machines, costumes, and dress forms, marveling over Rebecca's
design talent—and laughing at the abundance of
yellow sticky notes, some in odd locations. On
the coffeepot: "Err on the weak side." On the
bathroom door: "Jiggle the handle." On the draft-
ing-table lamp: "You're the best, Sis!"

Swinging doors led to the glorious showroom
and dressing rooms of Anytime Costumes. A
shiver of excitement slid up Meg's spine at the
new setting, eerily quiet and orderly compared to

the start of a school day. The seclusion was downright liberating. She'd forgotten how much she enjoyed her own company.

She hadn't told Rebecca that Trey had proposed. At first she'd convinced herself she didn't want to steal Rebecca's thunder. Meg's sister was obviously infatuated with her new beau, Michael Pierce—they couldn't take their eyes off each other.

But last night when she'd waved goodbye to Rebecca, Meg acknowledged that she wanted to keep Trey's proposal to herself in order to sort things out on her own, without anyone else's advice, no matter how well-intended. Kathie's parting remark about making sure Trey was the one for her had stuck in her mind like a trendy song. Not to mention the hurt in Trey's voice when she gently refused his offer to accompany her to Chicago.

If she was making a checklist of qualities she was looking for in a husband, Trey would score high. Handsome, polite, successful. They had similar tastes in books, films, politics. He was dependable—no, she would not say "boring"—and was always prompt for their Saturday-night dates and their Wednesday lunches. Friday evenings he usually spent with his father and two brothers in Mr. Carnegie's home office, smoking cigars and catching up on family business—real estate, transportation and petroleum.

On Sundays she joined his family for brunch at their vast home—Trey's brothers were both married, and everyone treated Meg as if she were already part of the family. The Carnegies had an opening, and she fit the mold—passably photogenic, suitably reserved and demurely successful. But she couldn't shake the feeling that Trey had picked *her* because of some real or imagined checklist, and not because she moved him. And worse—that she'd allowed herself to be picked.

She pushed aside her troubled thoughts, and her spirits rose as the colorful showroom became illuminated. Rebecca's costume shop was such a happy place, one couldn't help but be transformed—the perimeter of the showroom was lined with racks of costumes ranging from blue dinosaurs to Frankensteins to medieval maidens. Meg walked around, stroking the rich fabrics and exotic trims, admiring the more detailed costumes displayed on mannequins—a suit of "armor," characters from the Wizard of Oz, and an alien. The most elaborate costumes—an iridescent mermaid, an Indian chieftain, and many others were on dazzling display above the long counter.

Rebecca had also added a wall of performance costumes—spangled bodysuits, sequined halter tops, slinky pants, sheer skirts, high-slit gowns, and an array of showy accessories—shoes, hats, scarves. Even though she was alone, Meg looked all around before gingerly holding a blue sequined bikini up in front of her. She angled her head, smiling mischievously. Wouldn't everyone be scandalized if the Teacher of the Year showed up wearing something like this? Then she sighed and rehung the bikini—some women were born to wear sequins and some women were born to wear cotton.

Mirrors abounded. She knew her sister enjoyed dressing up to entertain customers. Although Meg couldn't bring herself to do the same, she had foregone her normal ''baggy'' dress in favor of jeans, T-shirt, and green V-neck sweater, all loose enough to conceal the curves her mother had convinced her eons ago would attract the wrong kind of attention. Since she'd inherited her mother's figure, she assumed her mother was referring to the type of man her father had been—the type of man who would love, then leave a woman with two small children. Maybe that's why she'd been drawn to Trey, to his…stability. And his relative indifference to her curves.

Unsure what the day would bring, she'd opted to French braid her fine-textured light brown hair into a single plait down her back to keep it out of her way. She squinted at her reflection—maybe she'd get a new hairstyle before she returned home, or even a complete makeover. Contact lenses? A new outfit? The more she thought about it, the more she wondered if she was simply bored with herself, and was allowing that boredom to overflow into other areas of her life. Somewhat cheered at her revelation, she turned her attention to opening the store.

Following a list of instructions Rebecca had left, as well as the numerous yellow sticky notes, Meg counted cash into the register, turned on the stereo beneath the counter, and flipped the sign on the door to Open. When she unlocked the front door of Anytime Costumes, she was startled by the ringing of the overhead bell.

"No bells," she muttered, vowing to tie up the brass clanger as soon as she found a ladder.

Humming to the oldies tune playing over the speakers, she pressed her nose against the window until her glasses bumped. The street was studded with cars. Two policemen rode by on horseback. The shops across the street—a bakery, a dry-cleaners, and an old-fashioned barbershop—were already open for business. A rounded woman sweeping the sidewalk took a good-natured swat at a kid going by on a scooter.

It was a cool, blustery Saturday in Chicago, but

the sky reminded her of a child's drawing—clear blue with white fluffy clouds and a radiating bright sun, still hanging low. Meg grinned and stretched tall on the toes of her tennis shoes, effused with a heady feeling of freedom, like the first day of summer vacation.

But the tinkle of the bell on the door cut short her reverie. She turned, blushing guiltily at being caught in the throes of giddiness. She was, after all, representing Rebecca's business.

"Hidy-ho!" A dark-skinned deliveryman walked in bearing a stack of packages and a friendly smile.

"Hello."

His smiled widened. "You must be Rebecca's sister from Peoria. She told me to expect you."

She smiled and stuck out her hand. "Meg Valentine."

"Hello, Meg Valentine. I'm Quincy Lyle. Welcome to Chicago."

"Thank you." She wasn't sure why, but she suspected the delivery man was gay. Maybe because he was so approachable—there was no filter of sexual attraction.

"Mighty good of you to look after the shop for Rebecca while she enjoys a few days away with Mr. Pierce."

"You know Michael?"

He pushed back his cap. "I know almost everyone around here. They make a great couple, don't they?"

"Yes, they do." Meg signed the clipboard he extended.

He gestured vaguely. "You know your way around the costume shop?"

"I've spent time here with Rebecca, but never on my own."

"Have you met Harry?"

She frowned. "Who?"

He gave a little laugh and a dismissive wave. "Never mind." He pulled a card from his pocket. "If you need help getting around town, or if you need anything at all, just call my cell phone number."

Meg smiled. "Thanks."

He nodded toward the street where more policemen on horseback had gathered. "I guess you heard about the local commotion."

"No."

"Big splashy benefit in town, lots of celebrities around."

Meg made a rueful noise. "I have a friend who's a celebrity hound—she'll be disappointed she missed a chance to spot someone famous and get their autograph."

"Do you have friends here in Chicago?"

"Not really."

He rooted in his back pocket. "I have an extra ticket to a reception tonight if you'd like to come. The hotel is just a couple of blocks from here. A lot of my friends are coming—it'll be fun."

She smiled. "Thanks. Maybe I'll do that."

"Bring your camera—with luck, you can bring your friend back a souvenir." He flashed a grin. "See you later."

Meg felt a rush of gratitude for Quincy's generosity, and his upbeat visit seemed to set the tone for the rest of the morning. The shop was a whirlwind of activity as customers returned costumes, and others came in to try on garment after garment looking for just the right one. Michael Pierce's restaurant, Incognito, had become a popular spot for dining in costume—according to Rebecca, every night was a masquerade party, and business was booming. The bell on the door rang incessantly, and Peoria seemed like a million miles away.

An attractive middle-aged woman named Mrs. Conrad came in with a tin of cream candy. She appeared to be a regular customer since she was familiar with the store layout. She rented a sexy cowgirl outfit, complete with a little rawhide whip. Just putting the items in a bag sent a blush to Meg's face.

Around lunch time, she got a breather. Meg sighed and sank onto a stool behind the counter, marveling at the business her sister had grown. She pulled off her glasses and massaged her temples, then used the hem of her sweater to clean the smudged lenses. The ringing of the bell on the door startled her and she dropped her glasses on the counter. While she fumbled for them blindly, the customers approached the counter—bright blotches of color, a man and a woman from the sound of their voices, and they seemed to be bickering. A hot flush climbed her neck and cheeks as she searched the counter in vain—she felt like Mr. Magoo.

"Are these what you're looking for?" the man asked, placing her glasses in her hands. He had a warm, pleasing voice.

"Thank you," she murmured, then jammed the glasses on her face. But just as her vision returned, her speech fled. Her helpful customer was tall, dark and exotic looking, tanned with dark hair and eyes, high cheekbones and a prominent nose. Around thirty, she guessed, although he had the carriage of a more mature man. Or maybe it was his sturdy build that made him look older, or the fact that he was dressed in black from head to toe. Regardless, she was sure she'd never seen anyone more handsome in her life. Quincy's comment about celebrities being in the area came back to her, and she wondered if he was someone she should recognize. Of course she couldn't ask him, because she couldn't speak.

"You're welcome," he said with a little smile, and he squinted at her, as if something weren't quite right. Were her glasses crooked? Her hair falling down? Drool spilling over her chin? Meg was paralyzed.

"Could I get some help, please?" his companion said in a high-pitched voice. The woman sounded annoyed.

Meg jumped up, an apology on her tongue. Until she got an eyeful of the blond bombshell. She blinked. "You're...Taylor...Gee."

The woman gave her a tight smile. "Smart kid. I'd like a private dressing room, please. And an ashtray, pronto."

4

KATHIE WOULD NOT BELIEVE this, she simply would not believe this! Feeling a little light-headed, Meg carried an armful of show costumes to the dressing room where she'd taken Taylor Gee. The brawny guy in black, some sort of body-guard she now realized, stood outside the curtain, his hands clasped behind him. He made it a point to be alert every time the door opened, but he didn't appear menacing. Still, she wondered what weapons he harbored under that jacket—a woman who looked like Taylor Gee probably attracted all kinds of weirdos. From the looks of him, though, he could probably handle just about anything....

He smiled as she approached and her throat went dry. "Should I knock?" she whispered.

"Go on in."

Oh, that voice. Meg swallowed and cleared her throat loudly before she opened the curtain a fraction of an inch and peered inside.

"Come in and close the curtain," the starlet said without looking up. She was punching in a number on a tiny purple cell phone with a pencil. Those three-inch-long nails had their limitations, Meg guessed.

She hesitated, hoping another customer didn't need her help right away. Rebecca hadn't left her cheat sheets for what to do when a megacelebrity stopped by. Maybe she should have put an Out To Lunch sign on the door.

"I'll let you know if you're needed out here," the man in black said.

She nodded gratefully, then entered the dressing room and closed the curtain behind her in one quick motion. She stood frozen, her arms full, while she waited to be acknowledged. Taylor Gee had made herself at home in the large red dressing room, scattering the contents of her purse— makeup, brushes, a bottle of water, coins, dollar bills, prescription bottles—over the upholstered cushions on the three benches that formed a U. She appeared to be conferring with a thick schedule book that lay open in front of her. A long thin cigarette dangled from her mouth. She took a drag and leaned her head back to exhale straight in the air just before she spoke into the phone.

"Jules, this is Taylor. I'm in town for a benefit, and *I* need the benefit of a facial."

The woman was too beautiful for words. Between her tangle of white-blond hair and her golden tan, she fairly glowed. She wore a pink suit with flowing pants and a matching sweater with a feather boa collar. Her shoes were black and pink zebra print stilettos. Everything about her oozed sensuality and femininity. In contrast, Meg felt like peeling wallpaper.

"Oh, I knew you would work me in! I'll see you around three-thirty. Love you, too, sweetie."

The offhand way the woman tossed around endearments made Meg feel backward. She didn't even have a pet name for Trey, the man who had *proposed* to her.

Taylor pushed down the antenna and bounced the phone on a cushion toward the pink leather bag that Meg assumed had cost a small fortune. She stood and kicked off her shoes as if they were discount knock-offs and took another drag on her cigarette. This, Meg realized, was when she should have told the woman that the fire marshal frowned upon smoking in retail businesses. But she didn't say anything because she suspected that even the fire marshal would make an exception for Taylor Gee.

"Did you bring everything I selected?"

Meg nodded, marveling that they were nearly eye-to-eye without Taylor's stilettos. Taylor Gee just seemed so much larger than life that Meg assumed she was taller than her own five feet seven inches. "Yes, and a few extra."

Taylor smiled, displaying a dazzling array of white teeth, but the smile didn't reach her eyes. "Good girl. Now hang those up and help me out of these clothes."

Meg did as she was told, although she hoped that the woman didn't expect her to, um, *watch.*

Taylor removed her jewelry and tossed it in a pile on a nearby cushion. Meg prayed nothing got lost.

"Unzip me, please."

Taylor turned her back and held up her glorious hair with one hand. Meg swallowed hard, then stepped forward to slide down the pull of the fine zipper. The feather collar and the cigarette smoke tickled her nostrils, but she would have imploded before she would have sneezed on the starlet's back.

The sweater came off—not an easy feat with Taylor still holding a lit cigarette—and landed in a far corner. She wore a sheer pink bra that was a little short of modest. Then she leaned over and stepped out of her pants. They landed opposite the sweater. Taylor turned and stood before her, a miniscule bra and a pink thong away from full disclosure.

Meg turned quickly and reached for the first

outfit, a body-glove dress made out of blue iridescent fabric. "My sister designs most of these pieces—" She stopped when the filmy pink bra when flying past her to land near the sweater.

Busying herself with removing the gown from its hanger, Meg turned her back and kept her eyes averted. But Taylor snatched the dress from her, and Meg couldn't help but get an eyeful of what had every man in America drooling.

Meg was no prude...she grew up with a sister, for heaven's sake. She'd seen other women naked. Sort of. At the shower room in college, in the steam room at the YMCA, in *National Geographic.* But there was a difference in nudity for the sake of practicality and nudity for the sake of, well...being seen.

The woman was well-endowed, all right. And perky. Incredibly perky.

Taylor bent over to step into the dress, and Meg was exposed to yet another angle of the woman's incredible body.

"I, um, think I hear another customer," Meg said, gesturing toward the curtain.

Taylor pulled the form-fitting dress over her breasts and snapped the straps into place. She frowned toward Meg. "Well, go if you must. But come back quickly." She reached into the neckline of the dress, grabbed her left breast and hefted it higher. The binding fabric of the dress held it in place. When she reached in to adjust her right breast, Meg fled.

JARETT TRIED NOT TO STARE at the young woman who emerged from the dressing room, but he had to satisfy his curiosity—was his imagination playing tricks on him, or did this bespectacled shop-girl bear a striking resemblance to Taylor?

It wasn't just the large eyes or the high cheek-bones or the chiseled nose that had struck him when he first walked in and saw her without her glasses. But throw in the full-blown mouth, the height, and the slender build, and she could be Taylor's cousin. And if the loose jeans and baggy sweater concealed what he suspected they concealed, she could be her *sister.*

At the moment, though, she was looking a little shell-shocked from her brief encounter with Taylor, and he could guess what had transpired in the dressing room. Taylor simply didn't understand the concept of modesty, while this poor girl looked as if she might have been valedictorian of her private Catholic school. Indeed, she was tugging at the neckline of her T-shirt, as if she could stretch it into becoming a turtleneck.

''I, um, thought I heard another customer,'' she said, scanning the vacant shop. She stabbed at her glasses in what he had observed, in the short time he'd been here, to be a nervous habit.

"It's okay," he said. "Taylor can be a little...overwhelming."

She tugged on her neckline again. "I'm still trying to adjust to the fact that she's even here. I mean, I thought celebrities had people to shop for them. And this isn't exactly Rodeo Drive."

"Taylor does what she pleases. Your display windows caught her eye. She won't mind if you say she was here if it will help your business, but I have to ask that you not say anything until she's gone. The press has been relentless lately."

She nodded, wide-eyed, as if the idea of revealing Taylor's whereabouts hadn't even occurred to her. Her naïveté was refreshing.

"I'm Jarett Miller," he said, for no other reason than he wanted to banish that deer-in-the-headlights look from her face.

"M-Meg Valentine," she said. "I assume you're Miss Gee's bodyguard."

He smiled at her formality. "And longtime friend."

A genuine smile curved her mouth. "I'm sure Miss Gee is glad to have someone close to her who she can trust. Would you like a cup of coffee, Mr. Miller?"

He'd been up most of the night with Taylor on

one of her crying jags. "That would be nice, thanks."

The intriguing sway of her retreat convinced him that, curve to curve, she could hold her own against Taylor. Funny how one woman with spectacular looks wound up on television, while another woman with spectacular looks wound up tucked away in a little retail shop.

Meg returned with one cup of black coffee.

"None for you?" he asked with a nod of thanks.

Her smile lit her beautiful green eyes, veiled behind the black-rim glasses. "Not on an empty stomach."

He checked his watch. "We're keeping you from your lunch."

"No, that's fine," she said with a musical laugh. "I'm grateful for the business. And flattered. My friends and I are big fans—we never miss *Many Moons*."

He couldn't explain the effect her quiet voice had on him. Everything about her was simple and elegant—her hairstyle, her clothing, the way she moved her hands, the carriage of her shoulders. Her precise enunciation told him she was scholarly. In fact, nothing about her demeanor lent itself to the kind of woman who would own a costume shop, but neither did she seem like the kind of woman who would settle for being a clerk in a costume shop.

Her hands were bare except for a ring on her right hand, a single pearl mounted in a simple gold setting. The type of ring a girl might receive as a graduation present from her parents. She wore an inexpensive, practical watch. It was hard to guess her age—maybe twenty-four or twenty-five? The fussy braid in her light brown hair added to her ethereal appearance. At first glance, Meg Valentine was almost...mousy, and the fact that he knew better made him feel as if he were in on a wicked secret. Explicably, he wanted to know everything about her, and for once, he wished his time was his own so he could ask her to dinner.

From inside the dressing room came an impatient sigh. "Is that girl out there finished with whatever she left to do? I could *use* some help."

At times he wanted to wring Taylor's neck for her rudeness, but she was like a tall, difficult child with no respect for anyone else's feelings. And a reprimand from him would send her into a downward spiral that he'd spent hours trying to cajole her out of. So, much like a weary father, he made excuses for her.

"She's tense about an appearance tonight for a children's benefit," he said in an apologetic voice. It wasn't far from the truth—as promised, Taylor hadn't taken any pills over the last twenty-four hours so she could be in top form tonight. But the lack of a mood-booster had left her irritable—more so than usual.

Meg nodded, her face soft with understanding. "I can't imagine how stressful it must be to be in her shoes for even one day."

"Am I talking to myself in here?" Taylor shouted.

Jarett gritted his teeth while Meg dashed back inside the dressing room. From the murmur of their voices, Meg's soft, pleasing one and Taylor's high-pitched grating one, it appeared that Taylor was delighting in bossing Meg around. In between customers, the poor girl left and returned to the dressing room a half-dozen times, her arms full of glittering clothing. Every time the curtain opened, a cloud of cigarette smoke billowed out.

An hour later, Meg left the dressing room for what he hoped was the last time. Taylor stuck her head out and gave him a sly grin. "Want to see?"

He opened his mouth to decline, but she grabbed his arm and yanked him inside. To prevent a scene, he set his jaw and humored her as she posed in a long red dress with a neckline that plunged to her navel, and a front slit that hit mid-thigh. "What do you think?"

"It's…nice," he agreed, coughing mildly into his hand. The cigarette smoke was as thick as fog.

She narrowed her eyes and with a wrenching twist, ripped the slit higher, high enough to reveal that she wasn't wearing panties. "What about now?"

He summoned all his patience. "I hope you have something more demure in mind to wear to the children's benefit tonight."

She frowned. "My publicist committed me to wearing a gown by a new designer, and it's absolutely horrid—it has sleeves, for heaven's sake."

His mouth twitched. "Imagine that. Are you ready to check out?"

She nodded to a pile of clothing on the cushions. "I'll take those. Would you take care of it for me, darling? And remember to buy every size in the shop."

To minimize the chance of someone else showing up in the same outfit. Taylor was nothing if not predictable.

"Sure," he said, picking up the clothes.

"Wait," she said, then lifted the red dress over her head. "I'll take this one, too." She tossed the garment on top of the pile, then stood in all her naked glory, a challenging light in her deep blue eyes. "Looks comfy enough in here to lie down, doesn't it, Jarett?"

Every now and then, he was reminded of Taylor's penchant for dangerous sex. Jarett's stomach turned. "Behave, Taylor. And get dressed."

He exited the dressing room and approached the counter where a young girl and her mother were buying pink satin gloves. Meg was smiling and talking to the girl, chatting about school and little-girl things. She seemed like a natural with children, and he wondered if she had any of her own.

"Goodbye," she said as her customers walked away. "Have fun at the dance."

He piled the clothes on the counter.

"Is Miss Gee finished shopping?"

He nodded, enchanted by her smile, and by the tiny stud earrings in the lobes of her ears. With as much diplomacy as possible, he explained about Taylor wanting to purchase every size available of the garments she'd picked. Meg blinked.

"That's going to be expensive."

"I'll be paying in cash."

She swallowed. "Okay. Give me a few minutes to wrap everything." She worked quickly, and when the total was tallied, she looked up with a little wrinkle between her eyebrows. "That will be f-fourteen th-thousand, one hundred and twenty-five dollars. And thirty-nine cents. Sir.''

He withdrew a thick wallet and counted out the money in large bills. ''Thank you for your hospitality to Taylor. And to me.''

She nodded, placing the bills in the cash register tray with shaking hands. ''You're very welcome.''

''Good luck, Meg Valentine.''

She looked up, and pushed her glasses higher. Her green eyes widened slightly and something...electrical passed in the air between them. Her lips parted, and a flush made her cheeks grow pink. She blinked rapidly and her chin jerked to the right, as if she were startled, or taken back.

''Jarett,'' Taylor said behind them, sounding irritated.

He turned. She had emerged from the dressing room, dressed, thank God, in her pink suit.

''Jarett, I need to be zipped up.'' She sighed and stomped up to him like a sulky teenager.

He complied, aware of Meg's eyes on them as he fumbled with the small zipper key. From the way she averted her gaze, she thought he and Taylor were lovers. And even though it wasn't the first time someone had thought as much, the fact that chaste little Meg Valentine with the braided hair and the big green eyes thought so suddenly mattered to him.

"Let's go," Taylor barked. "I'm having a facial in thirty minutes." She jammed on big, black sunglasses.

"Um, Miss Gee?" Meg asked.

Taylor lowered her sunglasses. "Yes?"

Meg blushed furiously. "I hate to bother you, but my girlfriend Kathie is a big fan of yours."

"And?" Taylor snapped.

Jarett wanted to shake her because Meg looked as if she might swallow her tongue. "Would you like an autograph to take to your friend?" Jarett asked.

"Y-yes," Meg said. "If it wouldn't be too much trouble, Miss Gee."

"It wouldn't be," Jarett said, giving Taylor a pointed look.

After a few seconds' hesitation, Taylor manufactured a smile. "Of course not." She whipped a folder out of her large pink purse and withdrew a publicity photo. "What's your friend's name?"

Meg smiled. "Kathie, with an I-E."

Taylor signed the head shot with a flourish and slid it across the counter. "I take it you're not a fan of mine?"

Taylor's trademark tact.

"Oh, no—I mean, yes, I am," Meg stammered. "I never miss your show."

Taylor finally smiled and pulled out another photo. "What's your name?"

"Meg. Meg Valentine."

"How sweet," Taylor said, not sounding very sweet. "Here you go, Meggie."

Meg bit into her lower lip and smiled. "Thank you very much, Miss Gee."

Without a word, Taylor turned and marched toward the door, managing to take up three times as much room as her slender form required. She had certainly mastered the art of the grand exit.

Jarett frowned, picked up the bags of clothing, and followed her, as he'd done a thousand times. But at the door, he felt compelled to turn back— something about the mousy little Meg called to him. Maybe she reminded him of the sweetness of the small town in West Virginia where he'd grown up. Maybe it had just been too long since he'd spent time with a genuine person. Whatever the appeal, he felt torn between his duty to shadow Taylor and a sudden desire to loiter with the shopgirl. A crazy impulse, he knew, but there it was.

"Yes, Mr. Miller?" she asked, her hand at her throat, tugging on her collar.

His mind raced—she had no idea the impression she'd made, which rendered it all the more profound. He felt like a colossal fool standing in the doorway, holding shopping bags and letting the cool breeze dilute the cozy warmth of the shop. "Perhaps our paths will cross again."

He wanted the words back as soon as they left his mouth. What an inane thing to say—of course their paths would never cross again.

But she was too nice to let on that he'd spoken utter nonsense. Instead, she pushed up her glasses and smiled. "Perhaps."

5

MEG TURNED the Closed sign on the door and exhaled slowly. Her limbs ached from the unaccustomed movement of taking down and rehanging heavy costumes. And another strange feeling had overtaken her since Jarett Miller had walked in and placed her glasses in her hands. It was an alien sensation of self-awareness, as if suddenly everything she said and did mattered. Ridiculous, since Jarett Miller probably wouldn't have noticed her if she'd sprouted wings and taken flight. Especially not while standing within a mile of Taylor Gee.

Taylor Gee, as in Gee Whiz. That woman gave a person an idea of what Eve, the original woman, might have looked like. Meg still couldn't believe she'd actually seen the star of *Many Moons* up close and personal—*very* personal. And Taylor Gee's life seemed just as glamorous as she'd imagined—arranging facials on the fly, spending money like water, and being protected by a hunky bodyguard.

Leaning back against the locked door, Meg absorbed the coolness of the metal and glass. If she had a league, Jarett Miller would be way out of it. But she could dream, couldn't she? Oh, she knew she was buying into the mystique of the brawny bodyguard dressed in black, but his sex appeal was wrapped up in more than his incredible looks—there was something about the warmth in his dark eyes, the friendliness in his voice, the way he engaged her in unnecessary conversation. If she closed her eyes, she could almost believe their paths *would* cross again.

Then a delicious thought materialized. With heart pounding, she pulled the ticket Quincy had given her from the pocket of her jeans. The hotel reception was for a children's benefit called A Book in Every Nook—the same one Taylor Gee would be attending? The charity was one of Meg's favorite literacy causes. And maybe she'd have a chance to talk to Jarett Miller again after all.

As her excitement grew, she glanced down at her casual clothes. She hadn't packed anything nice enough to wear to a swanky reception, but maybe there was something in the store—

Meg stopped halfway to the racks, a rueful laugh bubbling in her throat—her fantasies had run amuck. She had come to Chicago to contemplate Trey's proposal, and here she was spinning daydreams about the bodyguard of one of the most desirable women in the world. She hadn't missed the intimate exchange when Jarett had zipped Taylor's sweater. Hadn't he said they were longtime friends? Longtime lovers, more likely.

It was undoubtedly part of the man's job to pave the way for Taylor Gee wherever she traveled, even if it meant shmoozing with retail clerks so they wouldn't gossip to the media. Well, she had no intention of calling local reporters, but she suspected she would have the undivided attention of the girls in the teachers' lounge when she returned to school. She knew Kathie would flip over the autographed picture.

And her sister Rebecca would flip over the huge sale. Speaking of which, she needed to get the deposit ready to drop at the bank—just knowing she had so much cash on hand had left her nervous the rest of the afternoon.

She sighed and tore the reception ticket in two, then dropped it in the wastebasket behind the counter, chastising herself for allowing her imagination to run away with her. She would have a quiet dinner by herself, and maybe catch a movie. Plus she'd promised Trey that she'd call him tonight. And in between, she needed to do some serious thinking about the direction she wanted her life to take.

Which, she reminded herself sternly, had nothing remotely to do with Jarett Miller.

After carefully counting the day's receipts, she placed the money in a paper deposit envelope. Rebecca's notes had said the night deposit bags were in a box in the supply room. Meg found the supply room, and flipped on a light. The closet was filled with empty boxes, garment bags, printer paper, and props of all kinds. She located the nylon night deposit bags and removed one from the box, noting it was already tagged with the name of Rebecca's store and her account number. All Meg had to do was put the deposit and a deposit slip inside the bag, then place it in a drop box at the bank. Simple. She turned to leave the closet, then shrieked at the sight of a man standing behind the door.

Well, okay, he was a rubber man, but nearly lifesize and a bit frightening at first glance. The blow-up doll was dressed in blue-and-white-striped pajamas, and wore a yellow note pinned to his lapel. She squinted. Correction—make that a note to *her*. Perplexed, Meg removed the straight pin that held the message in place.

Meg

Meet Harry. Remember Angie's bachelorette party in college? We all agreed to pass Harry from one single friend to the next as we met and married the man of our dreams. Lana Martina (Healey) sent Harry to me a few weeks ago, just after my breakup with Dickie. She assured me that Harry is a good-luck love charm, although I had my doubts. But believe it or not, Harry was instrumental in bringing me and Michael together. I'm leaving you this note because I know you'll find it Saturday when you close the store. Harry is yours now, because—are you sitting down?—Michael and I are in Vegas. We've eloped.

Meg inhaled sharply—their mother would have a seizure. Her greatest fear was that her daughters would marry the wrong man. And while Michael Pierce seemed like an upstanding, successful guy, he and Rebecca had been dating for only a few weeks. What was her sister thinking?

I know you think I've lost my mind, Meg, but I can't explain how happy I am. I'd rather spend a day with Michael than a year with any other man. He has changed my life. By the time you read these words, I'll be

Mrs. Michael Pierce! I'll call you Sunday.
And I hope that Harry brings you as much
luck in love as he has brought me.

                              Love, Rebecca

Meg reread the note, then stared at Harry, who
sported a permanent grin and an erection that
tented his pajamas pants. She remembered the
party, but not this, this, this...*disfigured* balloon.
A good-luck love charm? Her sister had obviously
gone mad while working in the little fantasy
world she'd created in her shop. Hadn't Meg experienced firsthand how the fanciful place could
affect a person's thinking?

She frowned. Quincy had asked if she'd met
Harry—was he in on the myth too?

Meg lifted her hand in a little wave. "Nice to
meet you, Harry, but I have enough men in my
life. *Although...*" She pursed her mouth and
brushed a piece of fuzz from his sleeve. "My
friend Kathie might think you're cute, as long as
Principal O'Banion doesn't catch wind of you."
She smiled wryly, then wrinkled her nose and
sniffed.

Something was burning.

She swung around—a haze of smoke pene-
trated the showroom. She inhaled and her lungs
rebelled, forcing the smoke-filled air back up. She

coughed and covered her mouth, and, in the space of two seconds, a horrible realization dawned on her—the shop was on fire.

She ran for the phone and dialed 911, scanning for the source of the smoke. The red dressing room. An image of Taylor Gee's cigarette flashed in her mind—dropped and smoldering all this time? It seemed likely.

Meg's heart heaved in her chest. She rattled off the pertinent details to the emergency operator, then slammed down the phone. She yanked a scarf from a display and tied it around her nose and mouth, then grabbed the fire extinguisher from beneath the counter. If there was one thing that every elementary school teacher knew, it was how to put out a fire.

She pulled the ring on the canister as she ran for the dressing room, then threw open the curtain. Gray smoke billowed out—the upholstered cushions were on fire, and the bottom of the curtain had caught, but thankfully, the flames seemed to be contained. She aimed the nozzle and released a fire-choking stream of white powder at the base of the flames in a sweeping motion. The fire died rather quickly, but Meg emptied the canister to be sure.

The smoke alarm had been triggered, blaring incessantly into the store and the fire truck roared up just as she opened the door to begin airing out the shop. She pulled the scarf down from her nose and mouth and, in between coughing spasms, explained she was watching the store for the owner, her sister, who was out of town. Then she showed them where the fire had started, and stood back as four firemen double-checked her extinguishing handiwork and rooted in the debris for the source of the flame.

Meg was weak from the adrenaline rush, and congested from the smoke. She allowed herself to be led outside and examined, but was pronounced fine and given a glass of water to drink.

Fifteen minutes later, two firemen emerged, producing a charred bit of something they identified as a cigarette filter. Meg closed her eyes briefly—just as she suspected.

"Is this yours?" the older man asked with a frown.

"No."

"Customer?"

She nodded.

"Did you see the person smoking?"

She nodded.

His frown deepened. "Are you aware there's a no-smoking ordinance in public areas in this city?" For effect, he pointed to the sign posted in the window.

She hesitated, then nodded. "But the customer was someone famous, and…" The words sounded ridiculous even to her own ears, and the man in charge seemed to agree.

"The law applies to famous people, too, ma'am."

She felt like an idiot. But a lucky idiot considering Rebecca's entire business might have gone up in flames. She removed her glasses and rubbed her scratchy eyes with forefinger and thumb. *Surprise, sis, I burned your livelihood to the ground.*

The fireman stood with a clipboard, poised to write. "Do you want to press charges against the customer?"

Meg replaced her glasses and sighed. "No, it was my responsibility. I should have told her to put out the cigarette."

"Her?"

"The customer," she said pointedly, not about to reveal Taylor Gee's name.

He made a disapproving noise in his throat. "Okay. But you're mighty lucky the fire broke out before you left for the night."

Meg nodded and swallowed hard—especially considering she might have been asleep in the apartment over the shop. Her stomach rolled.

The fireman scratched his temple with the end

of a pen. "For insurance purposes, I need to know what was damaged, ma'am."

She shrugged slowly. "It was a dressing room, much like the other two."

He nodded, then scribbled on a form. "Looks like the damage is superficial—a little paint and putty, and you'll be back in business." Then he nodded toward the door. "But all those costumes will probably have to be cleaned to get rid of the smell."

Of course. She'd be forced to close the store for a couple of days. It was hard to predict how much business Rebecca might lose over her stupidity.

"And I have to warn you," he said, ripping off a duplicate of the report. "Your sister is probably getting reduced premiums because of the no-smoking ordinance. It's possible that the insurance company will refuse the claim, since a cigarette was involved."

Meg bit down on her tongue. It would probably cost a couple of thousand dollars to repair the dressing room, and heaven only knew how much more to have every costume in the showroom cleaned. Her hard-earned savings disintegrated in her mind, but she simply couldn't allow Rebecca to absorb the cost of Meg's mistake.

Another fireman emerged, holding the corner of

an unidentifiable object. "Found something else, Chief."

Meg squinted at the charred item, then her knees weakened. From the scrap of singed fabric, a hard plastic tag dangled, showing the name of Rebecca's shop and her account number.

Oh, God. She must have been holding the deposit when she charged into the dressing room with the fire extinguisher. And in the confusion, she'd dropped the bag.

Fifteen thousand dollars in cash...up in smoke.

6

"SO HOW'S MY LITTLE SIS?" David asked.

As always, Jarett was torn between telling the truth and breaking David's heart. And as always, he chose to spare his best friend. He leaned back in the stiff club chair and shot a look toward the closed door separating his hotel room from Taylor's. "Taylor is Taylor—she's on top of the world."

"I must have been bad luck," David said with a little laugh. "She struck gold as soon as I left L.A."

"It was just a matter of timing," Jarett assured him. But he wondered if David was hinting that he didn't want to come back to L.A. after his two-year stint in Haiti was over.

"I'm so proud of her," David said, his voice filled with brotherly love. "Tell her I got the video tapes of the show that she sent, but the camp barely has electricity, much less a VCR."

"I'll tell her," Jarett promised, doubting Taylor would understand. He was immediately contrite—

he'd promised himself that he'd stop being so cynical where Taylor was concerned. She had agreed to go cold turkey on the pills and booze, and so far, so good.

"And thanks for the care packages, Jarett—you don't know how much I look forward to them."

Jarett tried to imagine a place where a few magazines and toiletries offered such a reprieve.

"And the cash comes in handy, too. The children here work hard to help their families. I pay them to attend school so they can learn and still contribute to the household."

"Sounds rough, man."

"It is, but there's so much opportunity to do good here. I'm so busy, the days fly by. I can't believe I've been here almost a year."

"One down, one to go."

"Right," David said absently. "Listen, I have to run. Tell Taylor I'm sorry I missed her."

"I can wake her."

"No, let her rest. With her schedule, I'm sure she's exhausted."

Jarett bit his tongue.

"And Jarett, I can't say this enough—thanks for keeping an eye on Taylor. I know she can be a handful at times, but you always seemed to know how to handle her."

"She has all kinds of people now to handle her—her agent, her manager, her publicist."

"But those people are looking out for their best interests, not Taylor's. I know I can trust you to help keep her grounded."

Jarett squirmed. "I do my best."

"I know. Thank you, brother."

He was touched and honored that David considered him a brother. If the Gumms hadn't taken him in as a foster child and blended him with their own family, he had a good idea where his juvenile delinquent ways would have landed him. "You're welcome. Take care of yourself."

"I will. And I'll call when I can."

Jarett hung up the phone, filled with remorse. He didn't really have it so bad—guarding a beautiful celebrity, attending glamorous events, jet-setting to exotic locations. In fact, he suspected at least a million guys would gladly trade places with him. He'd made a promise to Taylor, and to her family, when he agreed to accompany her to L.A. to follow her dream. And he wasn't the kind of man who reneged on a promise when he got fed up. He nodded curtly, silently renewing his pledge to stick it out another year with Taylor, until she was more in control of her life.

He checked his watch—three hours until Taylor was expected at the benefit, but her publicist had ordered that she look wonderful, and be on her best behavior. The children's charity was a pet project of Mort Heckel, the president of the network airing *Many Moons,* and Mr. Heckel would be in attendance. Taylor had never met the man, so she was expected to make a good impression. And a little goodwill would go a long way to help her slightly tarnished reputation. Rosie had come along to help coordinate the hairstylist, the makeup artist, the wardrobe. In fact, he suspected she would be on the scene any moment.

He pushed himself up and walked to the door that separated the rooms. "Taylor," he said, rapping lightly. "Time to wake up."

He waited a few seconds, then opened the door and slipped inside the darkened room. The low buzz of Taylor's snoring sounded from the bed where she lay on her back. She had her days and nights mixed up, a side effect of the pills she'd been taking, he supposed. She was clad in pale pajamas, wearing a sleep mask over her eyes. Her wild hair was spread over the pillow, her mouth slightly ajar. The public would probably be surprised to know that the "it" girl of television snored. He smiled ruefully. Asleep, Taylor was childlike, almost angelic. A little like Meg Valentine.

The sweet shopgirl hadn't been far from his

mind since they left the costume place. Any shrink would probably tell him he'd projected onto the innocent woman all the things in life he thought he was missing out on. Meg Valentine didn't deserve to have that kind of burden dumped on her pretty head.

"Taylor," he said softly, reaching for the bedside lamp. But when the light came on, the first thing he saw was the bottle of pills, open. He scanned the prescription label. "Take one every eight hours as a sleep aid."

Oh, God. Frustration crowded his chest. He shook Taylor's shoulder.

She groaned and moved her head side to side.

"How many sleeping pills did you take, Taylor?" When she didn't respond, he shook her harder. "Taylor, tell me—how many did you take?" he repeated.

A knock on the door sounded. Rosie.

He strode over and yanked open the door. The little moon-faced woman jumped back. He shepherded her inside and closed the door. "Where in the hell did she get these?" he demanded, holding out the bottle.

Rosie moved from foot to foot. "I don't know."

He jammed his hand into his hair. "She's asleep and I don't know how many she took."

"It looks like a new prescription," Rosie offered.

He squinted at the label—it was. Taylor had had it filled yesterday, before they left L.A. And *after* she'd promised him she'd stop. The pill count read "12." He dumped the tiny white pills into his hand and counted ten. "She took two."

"Then she's going to be out for a while," Rosie said, biting her nails.

"She can't be," Jarett said. "She has to go to this benefit tonight and meet the president of the network."

"Short of having her stomach pumped," Rosie said, "I don't know what you can do. Even if you manage to get her on her feet, she'll be a zombie."

"I'm going to call Peterson. Try to get her under a cold shower, will you?"

Rosie blanched, but rolled up her sleeves.

Jarett went back to his room to call Taylor's agent, cursing under his breath with every step. She'd done it this time.

But his anger couldn't compare to Mac Peterson's.

"*What?* I can't believe she could be so bloody dim. You have to do something, Jarett."

"Rosie's working with her now, but I don't know how lucid she'll be."

Peterson sighed. "Well, we both know that no one expects her to be brilliant as long as she looks good for the cameras. But Mort Heckel expects her to be there. I'm not exaggerating, Jarett, when I say that this could be the difference between Taylor's contract being renewed, and her character stepping into an elevator shaft. He's caught wind of the rumors, and he doesn't want a diva on his hands."

Jarett massaged the bridge of his nose.

"Do whatever you have to do to get through this evening," Peterson said, his voice grave. "I'll be at your hotel first thing in the morning to have a serious talk with Taylor about her future in this business."

Peterson hung up, and Jarett let out the breath he hadn't realized he was holding. Hopefully Peterson could talk some sense into Taylor in the morning, but meanwhile, he had to think fast and pray hard.

Using his cell phone directory, he paged Taylor's official physician—a woman who refused to write gratuitous prescriptions. A few minutes later she returned his call. Jarett told her the situation and read the name of the drug from the bottle, and the strength in milligrams.

"Fluids will speed the drug through her system, but you have to have her cooperation for that.

Otherwise, she's simply going to have to sleep it off,'' the doctor told him. "She should be okay by morning. The good news is that if two pills knocked her out, she's not too far gone to come back with a little determination and rehab.''

"I'm trying to convince Taylor she needs to kick this thing before it ruins her life.''

The doctor sighed. "I applaud your efforts, but Taylor is going to have to come to that realization herself. Hang on and I'll give you the name of a discreet clinic in Chicago, just in case she decides to get help before she comes back to L.A.''

Jarett wrote down the information and thanked the doctor, then returned to Taylor's room, ever hopeful. Rosie had managed to get Taylor into the shower, but Taylor slumped against the tile wall, head lolling, eyes closed, still wearing her pajamas. Her faithful assistant propped her up under the stream of water, soaked to the skin herself. Rosie looked at Jarett. "She's not waking up— should we call a doctor?''

"I just did. She's not in danger, but she's going to have to sleep it off.''

"What about her appearance tonight?''

"I honestly don't know. Maybe she'll wake up in time to make a late entrance.''

He helped Rosie get Taylor out of the shower, and averted his eyes while the older woman removed the wet pajamas, toweled Taylor's limp body dry, and wrapped her in a terrycloth robe with the hotel's insignia. He carried Taylor back to the bed and tucked the covers around her. She sighed in her sleep and curled into a ball.

Jarett shook his head, wondering if and how he could save her from herself. He handed the prescription bottle to Rosie. "Flush these, and go through her things. If she brought anything with her stronger than aspirin, flush it too."

Rosie balked. "I'm not allowed to touch Miss Gee's things."

"I'll take full responsibility."

Rosie wrung her hands. "She's in trouble, isn't she, Mr. Miller?"

He nodded. "But we're going to help her."

"She can be so sweet sometimes," Rosie said, leaning over to brush Taylor's wet hair back from her temple. "It's almost like there are two of her."

Jarett nodded, but his mind raced ahead to this evening's event. How was he going to cover for Taylor this time? Say she had the flu? Had fallen and sprained her ankle? One part of him wanted to let her stumble and learn a valuable lesson, but another part of him wanted to prevent her from making a foolish mistake that could affect the rest of her career. And possibly, the rest of her life.

Suddenly, he looked up at Rosie, who was headed toward the bathroom with the pills. "I'm sorry, Rosie what did you say?"

Rosie shrugged. "I said she can be so sweet sometimes, it's almost like there are two of her."

Two of her. Jarett's heart beat faster as his brain tested the validity of the preposterous idea that occurred to him. Peterson's words came back to him.

No one expects her to be brilliant as long as she looks good for the cameras.

It couldn't possibly work…could it? With the right wig, makeup, clothes… Nah, they could never get away with it.

Then he looked back at Taylor, who made a mewling sound in her sleep. David's words rang in his ears. On the other hand, he had to at least try. And Mort Heckel had never met Taylor in person….

Jarett headed for the door. "When the hairstylist and makeup artist arrive, send them to my room. Make *certain* they don't see Taylor."

"Do you have an idea?" Rosie asked, her face hopeful.

"Yeah," he said with his hand on the doorknob, "but it'll take a goddamned miracle to pull it off."

7

MEG GULPED IN FRESH AIR and waved to the firemen as they drove away. She would not cry. When the governor had presented her with the Teacher of the Year award, hadn't he said the same word her colleagues usually used when describing her, *resourceful?* She tried to ignore the panic rising in her stomach. She would think of something. She had to.

"Meg!"

She turned, surprised to hear her name. Quincy Lyle climbed down from his brown delivery van and jogged across the street. "I heard about the fire—are you okay?"

She nodded, relieved to see a familiar face.

"You look exhausted," he said. "Let's go inside." He pushed open the shop door and steered her into the showroom. "What happened?"

Meg gestured toward the forlorn dressing room, where the scorched curtain hung and white powdery foam spilled out onto the floor. "A customer was smoking in the dressing room and left the cigarette. It must have smoldered for hours.''

''Was anyone hurt?''

''No, thank goodness. I had just closed up when I noticed the smoke. I managed to put out the fire with an extinguisher.''

He shook his head. ''Some people are idiots. Imagine leaving a cigarette burning?''

''It was my fault. I should have asked her to put it out.'' Meg sighed, feeling the weight of her stupidity.

''Do you know who it was? She should at least be held accountable for the damage she caused.''

''It was...Taylor Gee.''

Quincy's eyes bugged. ''The celebrity?''

Meg nodded miserably and walked behind the counter that was dusty with settled ash. She'd been so awed by the woman and her bodyguard, she'd taken complete leave of her senses. Like a star-struck adolescent. ''She bought a truckload of clothing and even paid cash.''

''Wow, I see your predicament. I'm a huge fan of hers.''

''Me too.'' She picked up the two signed photos, blew off the dust, and handed them across the counter. ''She signed one for my friend and one for me.''

He squinted at the autograph. ''Meggie?''

She shrugged.

"So what's the bitchiest woman on television like in real life?"

"Flamboyant, gorgeous."

He leaned into the counter, his eyes alight. "Is she a diva?"

Meg smiled—he wanted the dish. Quincy was definitely gay. "She wasn't exactly friendly," Meg said while wiping down the counter and the cash register. In truth, the woman had been a little...difficult. Then an image of Jarett Miller's face came to her. "But her bodyguard was nice."

He lifted an eyebrow. "Do tell."

Her faced warmed. "That's all—he was... nice."

"Did she have an entourage?"

"No, just the bodyguard. And they seemed close."

"You mean like lovers?"

She nodded.

"*Oh.*"

"But they also seemed mismatched."

"What do you mean?"

"I can't explain it—he just seemed very down to earth."

"Well, maybe Taylor Gee used to be down to earth too before she became a megastar. I think I read somewhere that she's from some little town in Kentucky or West Virginia or some place like that.''

Jarett had said he and Taylor were old friends—was he from a small town, too? It seemed to fit his no-nonsense look and attitude. And hadn't she detected a slight accent in his speech that had nothing to do with the west coast? She pushed aside her idle musings and finished dusting the bar. Then, glancing around the shop, she became depressed all over again.

"Taylor Gee will probably pay for the repairs," Quincy offered, "if for no other reason than to keep her name out of the papers. It couldn't cost more than a couple thousand to rebuild the dressing room."

"All the costumes will have to be cleaned, too."

"Ooh."

Meg pressed her fingers against her throbbing temples. "And it gets worse." Meg swallowed. "I dropped the day's deposit in the fire when I put it out."

"How much?"

Her stomach pitched. "Fifteen thousand in cash, plus a couple of checks."

He whistled low. "Maybe insurance will cover the loss."

"The fire chief said that the insurance claim

could be refused since the fire was caused by a cigarette.''

"Oh, right—the no-smoking ordinance." Quincy puffed out his cheeks. "Have you called Rebecca?"

"No."

"Don't want to ruin her vacation?"

"Honeymoon."

"Huh?"

She sighed. "Rebecca left me a note—she and Michael eloped in Vegas."

Quincy grinned. "That's great!"

She nodded absently, too distracted at the moment to dwell on her sister's hasty decision. "I can't very well ruin her honeymoon.... So that means I'll just have to get everything back in order before she comes home."

"Do you know where to find Taylor Gee?"

Meg sank her teeth into her lower lip. "Yes. She's going to make an appearance at the reception you gave me a ticket for."

He lifted both hands. "Problem solved. Take along a copy of the fire chief's report for backup."

Except her palms were sweating at the mere thought of having the awkward conversation with Taylor. *Hi, remember me? You nearly burned down my sister's costume shop. Do you have your checkbook handy?* And she was even more nervous at the prospect of seeing Jarett Miller again.

"What day is Rebecca returning?"

"A week from tomorrow."

He raised his hand. "So there's plenty of time to get things back the way they were." He pulled a small pad and a pen from his shirt pocket. "Here's the name of a contractor who can repair the dressing room. He freelances on the weekends, so he can probably start tomorrow. Tell him I gave you his number and he'll shoot you straight."

"Thank you, Quincy." She took a deep breath. One step at a time. "I'll go to the cleaners across the street and get an estimate for cleaning all the costumes."

"Good idea. Is there anything else I can do before I leave?"

She looked around. "You don't happen to know if Rebecca uses a cleaning service?"

"Jowers Commercial Cleaning, I'll bet. Most of the businesses around here use them."

"I'll check her Rolodex, thanks."

"Anything else?"

Meg shook her head. "That's all for now. You're a gem for coming by to check on me."

He winked. "We'll have fun tonight and it will

take your mind off things. Do you want a ride to the reception?''

"No, I'll meet you there." After she fished the ticket he'd given her from the trash and taped it back together.

"Okay. Chin up—at least no one was injured."

"Right," she said, managing a smile. But her stomach still ached over the unnecessary incident.

"I'll see you later."

Meg nodded, feeling marginally better as Quincy left the store with a wave. The bell on the door rang violently, and she rolled her eyes upward.

"*You* I can do something about," she muttered.

Meg grabbed a cloth and dragged a stool over to the door, then climbed up to silence the ringer. It was a petty little thing, she knew, to begrudge the sound of the tinkling bell, but the noise was driving her mad. An indication, she acknowledged wryly, of her tenuous state of mind.

Sticking the tip of her tongue out in concentration, she wrapped the small cloth around the ringer. But she didn't expect the door to swing open—too late, she realized she should have locked it. She clawed the air and screamed as the stool was knocked out from under her. In a split second, she pictured herself in a body cast, and tensed to hit the hard wooden floor.

Instead, she stopped, suspended in midair. Someone had caught her. Quincy. She straightened her glasses. No, not Quincy...

"Miss Valentine, I'm *so* sorry." Jarett Miller stared down into her face, his eyes wide with concern. "I didn't see you standing up there."

Meg couldn't speak. A hot flash of humiliation—and awareness—burned her skin. Her senses were thrown into overdrive by the musky smell of his leather jacket and the fact that he was holding her as if he were about to carry her over a threshold. She flailed, and he set her on her feet, then steadied her as she acclimated to being vertical again.

"Are you okay?" he asked.

She nodded and took a step back, pulling down the hem of her sweater.

He squinted and leaned forward, touching his thumb to her cheek. "What happened to your face?" He brought his thumb away and stared at the black, then turned to look around the shop, his gaze landing on the dressing room.

"There was a fire," she ventured.

He turned back to her, his jaw set. "In the dressing room Taylor used?"

She nodded.

His mouth flattened. "Was the fire caused by a cigarette?"

She nodded again.

He released a frustrated sigh. "Taylor's?"

"I believe so."

Jarett reached for his wallet. "How much damage?"

She stared at the wad of money he withdrew—this was going to be easier than she thought. "I—I'm not sure. I was going to get estimates."

"Will twenty thousand cover it?"

Meg blinked. Even though twenty thousand would probably cover the repairs *and* the missing deposit, she couldn't in good conscience accept more than the repairs cost. After all, she was the one who'd dropped the money in the fire. "I don't think—"

"Thirty thousand?"

Her jaw loosened, but she managed to lift her hand, stopping him. "You don't understand, Mr. Miller. The repairs and cleaning probably won't cost more than five thousand."

"But you must have something for your trouble."

He held out the thirty thousand dollars, and Meg's mouth went dry. The only time she'd ever seen that much money had been on a field trip to the Federal Reserve bank. All she had to do was take it, and her problems would be solved. Her fingers twitched.

Then she shook her head. ''No. I simply can't accept that much money.''

His dark eyes raked over her, and Meg suddenly realized how disheveled she must look—wrinkled clothes, smudged face, mussed hair. She also realized she hadn't asked an obvious question. ''If you didn't know about the fire, Mr. Miller, why did you come back?''

He pulled his free hand down his face and his fingers rasped over his square jaw, darkened with five-o'clock shadow. It suited him in his all-black attire, and for an instant, Meg got a glimpse of how menacing he might be if he had to protect the person in his charge.

Meg's heart beat faster. Had he come back to see her? To talk to her? Perhaps she hadn't imagined the connection they'd shared when he'd spoken to her earlier.

''I came back to ask a favor,'' he said, his voice threaded with remorse. ''Actually, it's for Taylor, but under the circumstances, I don't believe my timing is so good.''

Embarrassment flooded her—had Meg really thought the gorgeous man who protected Taylor Gee had come back just to see *her?* Even though she wanted to fall through the floor, she snatched a smile from thin air. ''No, that's fine.'' She smoothed a strand of loose, smoky hair behind her ear. "What do you need? Another outfit, a different size?"

"No, it's a little more complicated than that."

"What, then?"

He seemed to be studying her face.

"I'm a mess," she murmured, adjusting her glasses.

"No, you're perfect."

She looked up, and her pulse spiked. "Hmm?"

"Miss Valentine, has anyone ever remarked how much you resemble Taylor?"

She gave a little laugh. "My girlfriends think so, but they're not the most stable group of women I know."

"Taylor is ill," he said. "And I was hoping…that is, I was going to ask…what I mean is…"

"Yes, Mr. Miller?"

"Please, call me Jarett." He inhaled deeply, his broad chest expanding. "Taylor is expected to make a very important appearance tonight, and she can't. My question is, would you consider standing in for Taylor?"

Meg frowned. "Standing in? You mean, as her spokesperson or something?"

"No," he said, running a finger around his collar. "I mean…as Taylor."

Her brain chugged away, trying to make sense of his words.

"You two could be sisters," Jarett said. "I thought so the minute I walked in and saw you without your glasses. With the right hair and makeup, I think you could pull it off."

A few seconds passed before his words sunk in, then Meg swallowed hard. "You want me to…to dress up like Taylor Gee and…and pretend to be *her?*"

He nodded. "It goes without saying that Taylor would be in your debt."

She couldn't believe her ears. "You're kidding, right?"

He shook his head, his dark eyes serious. "And I would never suggest such a thing if the situation weren't dire."

Meg simply stared.

"You'd only have to make an appearance, and wave to the crowd," he continued. "Everyone will think you're Taylor—they won't have a reason to believe otherwise."

She plucked at the collar of her T-shirt again. "Oh, my God, you *are* serious."

He nodded slowly. "We'll make it worth your time, Miss Valentine." He held out the thirty thousand dollars.

Meg's mind raced. Thirty thousand dollars to

dress up like Taylor Gee for one evening. She wouldn't even consider such a preposterous arrangement, except it wasn't every day that she turned a pile of cash into a pile of ash. Taylor Gee could make good on the damage she'd wrought, and Meg would feel as if she were meeting the star in the middle. But...*dress up like Taylor Gee for one evening?* Absurd.

"Mr. Miller, Jarett, I'm sorry, but there's no way anyone is going to believe that *I* am Taylor Gee."

"We could at least try it," he coaxed. "And if it doesn't work out, then we'll call the whole thing off. Either way, you can keep the money."

The proposition was tempting, but...

"Jarett, you and I both know that it's more than just hair and makeup," Meg said, her cheeks flaming. "Everyone expects Taylor Gee to be...well..." She gestured in vague circles.

"Sexy?" he asked with a little smile.

She suddenly didn't know what to do with her hands.

"I'll help you," Jarett said.

A charge bolted through Meg, reminiscent of the adrenaline surge she'd experienced while putting out the fire.

He blanched, as if he just realized what he'd

said. "I mean, I'll get people to help you...feel more comfortable."

"Who else would know about this?" Meg asked. She couldn't believe she was even considering it. But for some reason, she wanted to please this man.

"Besides me, only Taylor's assistant," he said. "The hairstylist and makeup artist are local, and they've never met Taylor. We'll simply give them a photo to work from. If we can fool them, then we know we're okay." He cleared his throat mildly. "And of course, you couldn't tell anyone."

Meg frowned. "*If* I agreed to this outlandish scheme, Mr. Miller, I assure you that my lips would be sealed."

His face lit up. "So you'll do it?"

Meg conceded that she'd consider doing almost anything to make the man smile like that again. His eyes sparkled, and dimples appeared high on his cheeks. Quite unexpected in such a masculine face. And quite riveting.

"Meg?" he asked softly.

Her mother had once told her and Rebecca that she'd fallen in love with their father because of the way he said her name, as if he were the first person to see her as the woman she really was. Meg suddenly knew what her mother meant.

Jarett Miller was the first man who'd ever looked past her glasses and boring clothes to see the woman underneath. Okay, she acknowledged wryly, the woman he saw looked like Taylor Gee, but still…

"Meg, will you do it? I would be indebted to you, too."

For helping his lover, she realized with a start. A sobering reminder to keep her fantasies in check. "B-but I can't get around without my glasses," she protested.

"We'll get you blue contact lenses."

"On such short notice?"

"Yes."

"But my hair…"

"Would you consider a temporary color change? Something that would wash out?"

When she toyed with the idea of a makeover earlier, this wasn't exactly what she had in mind. But if she could look normal again by the time she left Chicago… Kathie's words came back to her. *Wouldn't it be grand to live in a celebrity's shoes for a few days…*

Jarett Miller's handsome face was tinged with desperation. She still had serious doubts about whether they could make her look like the larger-than-life starlet, but she had to admit that the lure of working with him, even for a few hours, was irresistible.

A low hum of excitement began to build in her midsection. How many women were given the chance to be a gorgeous sex kitten for an evening? And hadn't she been yearning for a change? And best of all—no one would know. It would be her delicious little lifelong secret, that Megan Leigh Valentine wasn't just the mousy Teacher of the Year.

"Meg?" he prodded, his voice hopeful.

Heady feminine power surged in her chest. "Okay, Jarett. I'll do it."

8

When Meg approached the door bearing the room number Jarett had given her, she suddenly realized why she'd never been accused of being impetuous, spontaneous or impulsive. Because she was no good at it.

She knew this appearance was important. She'd gotten a hint of what was at stake when Jarett instructed her to take the freight elevator to the twelfth floor when she arrived.

"Don't ask for directions, don't speak to anyone. Call me if you have any trouble," he said. "The reporters would have a field day with this story."

More than he knew. Meg pictured the headline: Teacher Of The Year Impersonates Taylor Gee— Badly! and she thought she might be sick. She hesitated, debating whether to turn on her heel and run. After all, she already had the money— twenty thousand instead of the thirty he'd offered, just enough to save her skin.

Then she sighed. No, she couldn't simply take

the money and leave the starlet in the lurch. Jarett either, for that matter. He must love Taylor very much to go to this much trouble finding a body double.

She smoothed a hand down the loose khaki-colored dress she'd donned after a hasty shower. Her hair was still damp, and her makeup nonexistent, but Jarett had insisted that time was of the essence. Grooming had taken a back seat to visiting the drycleaners across the street and contacting the man Quincy had told her about to make arrangements for repairs to the shop. But suddenly Meg wished she'd taken more pains with her appearance.

She rapped on the door lightly, deciding if no one answered, then she would have done her duty. But the door swung open to reveal Jarett, without the black leather jacket. A long-sleeve black knit shirt fit him snugly, hinting of the toned torso beneath. It was tucked into flat-front black slacks, hinting of—no, she wasn't going there.

"Hi," he said warmly. "I was afraid you would change your mind."

"I did," she admitted. "About a dozen times."

He smiled. "Come on in. Rosie should be here soon." He closed the door behind them. "She's picking up the hair dye and the contact lenses.

Good thing we managed to get a copy of your prescription from your optometrist.''

The foyer of the suite gave way to a large bathroom on the left, complete with separate vanity area, then a small galley kitchen, a breakfast bar, a sitting area, and a king-size bed in the far end, near the window. Meg practically gawked at the luxurious furniture and the spacious layout. ''Whose room is this?''

''Mine,'' Jarett said casually. He opened the refrigerator. ''Can I get you something to drink?''

Panic roiled in her stomach—she was in way over her head. How incredibly stupid to come to this man's hotel room. She didn't know him, not really, and she hadn't told a single soul where she was. How many times had she admonished her seven-year-olds not to talk to strangers? Maybe this was his game—traveling from city to city, scamming Taylor Gee lookalikes and ravishing them in his hotel room. If Jarett—was that even his real name?—decided to get rid of her, Meg would be a Jane Doe in the morgue until Rebecca got back from her honeymoon and missed her.

She watched him move with animal-like precision, the muscles in his back responding to the tiniest shift in position. He probably knew how to kill people with his thumb. Wasn't he at this very moment trying to ply her with liquor? She judged the distance to the door, and wondered if she could get to it before he caught up with her. The only weapon she had with her was a bottle of hair spray, although she *had* heard about a woman who'd used her eyeglasses to stab an assailant in the neck.

"I have root beer and lemonade," he said, holding up two bottles.

Oh. Her worries shriveled. "Root beer," she said, feeling like an idiot all over again. Jarett Miller had been nothing but a gentleman.

"Have a seat," he said, nodding toward the overstuffed chairs flanking a glass-topped coffee table. "I'll fill you in on some details while we wait on Rosie."

She sat, her heart beating double-time, her gaze inexplicably drawn to the king-size bed across the room. He didn't share a room with Taylor? Then she spotted the connecting door. Ah….

Jarett carried two bottles of root beer to the table and handed her one. "I can order you something from room service if you like."

The idea of solid food made her nauseous. "This is fine, thank you." She took a drink and held the sweet nutty taste on her tongue for a few seconds. Funny—she loved root beer, but she never thought about buying it when she did her grocery shopping every Sunday afternoon. Why would she deny herself such a small pleasure? she suddenly wondered. And did she do the same in other areas of her life?

Jarett sat down opposite her, and Meg realized that her left eye had developed a nervous tic. She pressed her finger against the twitch as unobtrusively as possible. "You never said what Miss Gee is suffering from."

He lowered his bottle and swallowed. "It's some kind of bug, but the doctor said she'd be better once she got some rest."

Meg nodded sympathetically. The woman's immune system was probably compromised from traveling and exhaustion. She couldn't imagine how hectic a celebrity's life must be. "What's so important about tonight's benefit that she has to make an appearance?"

"The children's charity is the pet project of Mort Heckel, the president of the network. He's going to be there, and he expects Taylor to be there, too."

Meg choked on the mouthful of root beer. "Will she, er, will *I* have to speak to him?"

"Possibly. But he's never met Taylor before so he won't know what to expect." At the knock on the door, Jarett said, "Excuse me," then went to answer it.

Meg sat frozen—she was expected to converse with Taylor Gee's boss? Coherently?

A short round-faced woman with jet black hair bustled into the room holding several bags and peered at Meg as if she were an animal in a zoo. "I'm Rosie Grant."

"I'm Meg Valentine."

The woman turned to Jarett and shook her head. "I don't know, Jarett. I can't see it."

"Meg," he said, "would you please remove your glasses?"

She did, and stared at the fuzzy pair. The little woman circled her. "My goodness, the resemblance *is* rather remarkable, isn't it?"

"Yes," Jarett said softly, and Meg blushed at the thought of his gaze sweeping over her. She'd never been scrutinized quite so thoroughly. Especially by such a handsome man.

"What are your measurements, Miss Valentine?" Rosie asked.

Meg blinked. "I, um…"

"She'll be fine," Jarett said quickly, in a voice that made Meg wonder just how much he'd discovered when he'd caught her in midair. Suddenly she was glad she couldn't see his face.

He clapped his hands together, as if changing the subject. "Meg, are you ready to get started?

The hairdresser and makeup artist will be here soon.''

She jammed her glasses back on her face. ''I suppose so.''

''Then I'll leave you in Rosie's capable hands while I check on Taylor.''

Her nervousness increased tenfold as he walked away, which told her just how much she was relying on Jarett to get her through this charade. He disappeared through the connecting door to the darkened room on the other side. A foreign sensation plucked at Meg when she thought about his devotion to Taylor Gee. Jealousy? How would it feel to have a man like Jarett Miller seeing to your welfare?

Trey's face appeared in her head—he made her feel safe, all right, but now she wondered if the security she felt when she was with Trey had more to do with his family stature and financial stability than the man himself. She shook her head slightly. It wasn't fair to compare the two men, Meg told herself. Any more than it would be fair of Jarett to compare her to Taylor. A sobering thought.

''Don't look so worried,'' Rosie said with a shaky smile, pulling Meg toward the bathroom. ''This will be...fun.''

Meg wasn't so sure, but in for a penny, in for

a pound. She allowed the woman to wet her freshly washed hair and apply the strong-scented colorant. While she sat in the vanity area and waited for the chemical to work, Meg watched the woman dart around, unpacking a range of products—contact lenses, skin bronzer, fake nails, body makeup. Rosie was a bit high-strung.

"Have you done anything like this before?" Meg asked.

"Goodness, no. This is an emergency."

"Well, I hope Miss Gee is feeling better soon."

"She will be," Rosie said, fluttering about. "After she deals with her little problem."

"Problem?"

Rosie stopped, wide-eyed. "Didn't Jarett tell you?"

"He told me that Miss Gee has a bug of some kind, and that she'll be feeling better in the morning."

"Oh. Yes, she does. And a problem with... allergies."

Meg nodded. "I'm allergic to ragweed. I feel for her."

"Well, now, let's get these contact lenses in," Rosie said, fidgeting. "The doctor gave me two different kinds in your prescription in case one is more comfortable than the other."

Meg had had plenty of opportunities to get contact lenses over the years, but she'd clung to her glasses out of familiarity and security. She'd gotten her first pair at the age of eight, and aside from bringing the world into focus, she'd discovered she could retreat behind them if need be. They were both a badge and a shield—girls assumed she was smart and boys assumed she was uninteresting. And as the years passed, she'd grown accustomed to the weight of the frames on her nose. There was something so...*naked* about exposing her bare face to the world.

Yet she was pleasantly surprised at how comfortable the contact lenses were. Everything seemed larger, the colors more vivid. And seeing herself with blue eyes was a shock.

But not as much of a shock as seeing herself with white-blond hair. Rosie dried and fluffed while Meg stared at the stranger in the mirror. She looked years younger and...dare she think it? *Sexy.*

While she marveled at the transformation, the red nails were glued on and filed down to one inch at Meg's request.

"Is it safe to enter?" Jarett's voice sounded through the door.

"Yes," Rosie sang, filing away.

Meg's heart jumped as Jarett came to stand behind her chair. He seemed to study every inch of her. His eyes held a strange light, and he seemed far away. Her pulse throbbed in her ears. After a long pause, he nodded slowly.

"Until this moment, I don't think I believed it myself, but by God, Meg, you're going to pull this off."

Panic flooded her anew as the unknown stretched before her. "But I don't know what to do or say when I get there."

"I'll brief you later," he assured her. "Don't worry, I won't leave your side."

She met his dark gaze in the mirror, and the same energy that had passed between them in the shop reverberated between them in the reflection. Her body reacted to the sound of his voice. Her skin sang with awakened nerve endings. She'd never felt so close to the edge of reason...and she'd never felt more aware of herself as a woman.

Behind her, his hand inched toward her hair. But just before he touched her, a knock sounded at the door, and the moment was gone.

"That will be our reinforcements," he said. "Rosie, the dress and shoes are in my closet, as well as some other bits of clothing."

"Yes, sir."

He produced a spectacular color headshot of Taylor. "Here's something for the makeup artist

and the hairstylist to go by.'' Then he looked back
to Meg.

''Meg, from this moment on, you are Taylor,
and that's how we'll address you. These people
are professionals that the network uses regularly,
although they've never worked with Taylor before. They're trained to not engage in personal
conversation with the celebrities they service, but
for insurance, I've explained to the agency that
Taylor's voice is strained, and that she is—I
mean, *you are* under doctor's orders to save your
voice for tonight.''

Meg sighed with relief—a respite before she
was required to perform.

''Rosie,'' Jarett said. ''I need to make a security sweep of the hotel where we'll be going tonight. I'll be back in an hour and a half with a
limo to pick up Taylor. Meanwhile, keep all the
doors locked.''

A look that Meg couldn't interpret passed between Rosie and Jarett, then Rosie nodded. Jarett
gave Meg a salute and a little smile. ''See you in
a little while...Taylor.''

Meg tried to smile, but her face was frozen in
fear. How had she gotten herself into this? The
gag would be over when the hairdresser and
makeup artist walked in and burst out laughing.

"No, really," they would say, "where is Taylor?"

"Put this on," Rosie said, handing her a white terry cloth robe to wear over her drab dress. Good thinking, Meg decided, kicking off her low-heeled shoes. Taylor Gee probably didn't own anything that could be called neutral.

She heard Jarett open the door and greet the visitors. Two female voices reached her ears. As their voices grew louder, Meg thought she might pass out, but Rosie gave her a reassuring pat. When the women appeared to Meg's left, she turned and presented them with what she hoped was a Hollywood smile.

"Taylor," Jarett said, giving her an encouraging nod. "Meet Paris and Tori. I explained about your voice."

Meg gave them a nod, and the two women, both of them young and attractive, practically curtsied.

"It's a pleasure to meet you, Miss Gee," said Paris. She held a suitcase which Meg assumed contained makeup.

"I'm such a big fan," Tori said, beaming. She carried a shoulder satchel brimming with hair implements.

Meg smiled and shook both of the women's

hands, mindful of the nails she was unaccustomed to wearing.

"Ladies," Jarett said cheerfully, shooting Meg an "I-told-you-so" look in the mirror. "I'll leave you to your jobs. Taylor, I'll be back in an hour or so."

When she acknowledged him with a little smile, he angled his head and held her hostage for a few extra seconds. She could get lost in that gaze, Meg decided, and finally tore her gaze away.

From the corner of her eye, she saw him leave. She didn't have time to digest the meaning of his glances because she was soon swept up in the world of powder puffs and curling irons.

"You're not as tanned as I thought you'd be, Miss Gee," Paris said shyly. "I hope I brought the right color palette."

Meg balked, but Rosie didn't miss a beat. "Miss Gee prefers bronzers to sun exposure." Then she produced a box of the brown powder she'd purchased.

"Much better for the skin," Paris agreed, then pursed her mouth when she saw the brand on the box. "And this is the best stuff in the industry." Then she set to work giving Meg the same golden glow that Taylor sported year around.

"Your hair is in marvelous shape," Tori said,

feeling the texture. "Very healthy. But would you mind if I cut off a few split ends?"

Meg indicated that she didn't mind.

"No more than an inch," Rosie warned.

Paris squinted in the mirror, then looked back and forth between Meg and the picture of Taylor. "Hmm."

Meg's stomach squeezed.

"What?" Rosie asked.

"I'll need to shape up the eyebrows," the woman said.

Meg exhaled in relief.

"Fine," Rosie said, fluttering her hands.

"And I brought false eyelashes because I heard that you like them, Miss Gee, but honestly, I don't think you need them."

"And isn't her skin amazing?" Tori asked.

"Yes," Paris agreed. "So fresh—as if you've never worn makeup."

Rosie cleared her throat. "We're in a bit of a hurry," she reminded them.

The women got to work and Meg succumbed to their ministrations for forty-five minutes. They were masters, she decided, amazed at the number of sins loose powder could conceal. She was dabbed and stroked and swabbed and patted and dusted and gelled and sprayed until the two professionals finally announced she was finished.

Meg stared in the mirror, astounded and a little frightened that nothing of Meg Valentine remained. Hair, eyes, makeup. She was, for all intents and purposes, Taylor Gee.

"Amazing," Rosie murmured.

"She is, isn't she?" the clueless makeup artist said.

"Beautiful," the hairdresser agreed. "But that's why you're the most famous actress on television."

"Thank you," Rosie said, shooing the women on their way. "And Taylor thanks you, too."

The women gushed and waved, and Meg waved back, mildly distracted by her own red nails. How did Taylor wear these things?

Rosie scampered back, hopping in joy. "They fell for it—they actually believed you were Taylor!" The woman looked over Meg's shoulder in the mirror. "I swear, I could almost believe it myself." Then she stood abruptly. "The only thing that remains is the dress." She whipped a garment bag out from the closet.

Meg turned and waited, her mouth completely dry. Rosie pulled out a long glittery teal green gown, long sleeved, with a slit on the side. It was a beautiful color. Trouble was, it looked as if it was sized for a child.

"It's too small," Meg croaked.

"It stretches," Rosie assured her. "Come on, off with your dress."

Meg closed her eyes briefly and tossed up a prayer.

9

JARETT TOOK A DEEP BREATH as he stepped off
the elevator and headed back to the room where
he'd left Meg Valentine. Images from his sweep
through the hotel where the children's charity reception was to take place left a stone in his stomach. Reporters had already gathered, more than
he'd seen since the Emmy Awards show. And
fans toting We Love Taylor signs were already
pushing at the barriers the police had erected.

Taylor's character, Tess Canton, had become a
bit of a cult figure with her outrageous clothes and
venomous mouth. Taylor's fans often showed up
at events dressed as her character, although, Jarett
conceded, the gap between Taylor and the character she played seemed to be closing.

Take that see-through yellow dress she'd worn
to the MTV Music Awards. When she stepped out
on the stage to present a statue, cameramen had
to scramble to keep the shot censor-friendly. She
hadn't told him about the dress she'd changed into
just before she stepped onstage because she knew

Jarett would never have let her wear it—for her safety's sake, of course. Sure enough, he'd barely been able to shield her from her mob of admirers when they left the ceremony that night. Taylor had loved the controversy, but she'd created a security nightmare. When he'd chastised her later, she'd pouted, saying she'd only worn it to get his attention. In typical Taylor-style, she'd stripped off the dress and flung it at him, flaunting her breasts with nipples rouged for the occasion. Jarett had kept the dress, in case she was tempted to wear it again, and pressed Taylor's publicity manager, Sheila Waterson, to find a stylist to make wardrobe decisions for Taylor. Of course, Taylor had already fired two stylists.

Meanwhile, the yellow dress had become a wildly popular subject among the late-night comedians, and, apparently, a staple in transvestite stage shows. He'd counted at least a dozen look-alikes milling in the crowd in front of the hotel, some of them sporting Adam's apples. The entire scene struck him as exceedingly sordid, and he suddenly regretted dragging Meg Valentine into the situation.

The poor woman didn't realize what she was getting into. In truth, *he* hadn't realized what he was getting her into, although he should have figured that Taylor's first public appearance since she'd been escorted out of Zago's restaurant for flashing patrons would attract a lot of media attention. He would have to stick especially close to Meg tonight, to shield her from both the crazies and the paparazzi. It wouldn't be a chore, he acknowledged, spending time with sweet, sexy Meg. He just wished it were under other circumstances.

Jarett stopped at Taylor's room door first and slipped inside. She hadn't moved since he'd last checked in on her, and her buzzing snore was a comfort to him—he'd begun to worry that she'd taken more pills than he thought. But her condition seemed to confirm what the doctor suggested—she'd just have to sleep it off.

Jarett leaned over the bed and pulled the blanket up to cover her exposed shoulder. ''You're going to be the death of both of us,'' he whispered. ''We need to get you well.''

She didn't stir, which was good since Jarett harbored a secret dread of Taylor's reaction when she found out that he'd arranged for a body double, a body double Taylor herself had considered mousy. He sighed and left the room to see what kind of transformation had occurred in his absence.

He knocked on the door to his room, thinking he still had time to call off this entire charade. He could send word that Taylor had the flu. People got the flu all the time, and celebrities were no exception. Taylor would simply have to suffer the consequences of her absence. And Meg would be spared the ordeal of what lay ahead of her tonight.

The door swung open and Taylor stood in the doorway, looking regal in a form-fitting teal gown. Then Jarett blinked. No, not Taylor.

"Meg?" he whispered, stunned at the complete transformation.

"Why, Jarett," she said in Taylor's soft Southern voice. "Don't you know me? It's Taylor."

Her white-blond hair had been wound up into some kind of complicated twist that he'd never seen Taylor wear, but it suited her immensely. Very classy. The dress covered a lot of skin, but the form-fitting fabric adapted to every curve.

And did the lady ever have curves!

"Why are you standing in the hall?" She extended her hand, tipped with long red fingernails, and tugged him inside.

Jarett went willingly. When the door closed behind him, Meg laughed, clearly pleased with herself. "What do you think?"

"I'm astonished," he admitted with a grin. And not completely unaffected, he realized suddenly. Meg Valentine had a figure to stop traffic, as voluptuous as Taylor's, but with more pleasing transitions. Her shoulders and arms were sculpted versus skinny, her breasts rounded versus jutting, her waist nipped versus cinched, her hips flared versus full. Meg looked the same way that Taylor might look if she took better care of herself.

When he glanced back to her face, he flushed. "I was staring, I'm sorry."

A smile curved Meg's lips. "Since you're staring at Taylor, I don't mind."

Jarett inhaled sharply—there it was again. That little pain in his chest when Meg looked at him as if she could see inside him. And suddenly he realized that no matter how much Meg looked like Taylor, she would always have her own eyes— even behind the blue contact lenses, they sparkled with an intensity that made a person feel important and connected.

Except the only thing between him and Meg Valentine, he reminded himself, was a short-term business agreement. Unfortunately. He cleared his throat and averted his eyes. "Where's Rosie?"

"She went back to her room to clean up. Don't worry—I was under strict orders not to open the door to anyone but you." Then she coughed mildly. "And she said to tell you that she would be staying with Taylor tonight so you could get some sleep."

Jarett tried not to frown—the woman made it sound as if he stayed with Taylor every night.

"Jarett," she said softly. "Isn't Taylor interested in seeing if I look like her? I thought she might want to give her approval, since I'm going on her behalf."

His gut clenched. Of course she thought she was doing this with Taylor's full approval, or else she wouldn't have considered going through with the charade. Because that was the way Meg Valentine with her braided hair and her little stud earrings was wired. He, on the other hand, had apparently become more like the jaded people in the entertainment industry than he realized.

"Taylor is asleep," he said carefully, avoiding telling a blatant lie. "But believe me, she'll thank you. Someday." He hoped.

Meg smiled, satisfied, and her simple trust touched him. He hated himself for deceiving her, but rationalized that she was being paid about fifteen thousand more than the repairs would cost. He had no idea how lucrative the costume business was, but fifteen grand for one night's work wasn't a bad paycheck in his book.

"Let me take a quick shower and change," he said. "Then we'll be on our way."

Her smiled wavered. "Okay."

She felt awkward, he realized, being in a man's

hotel room while he showered. In the no-holds-barred atmosphere of L.A., he'd almost forgotten what modesty looked like—it was very refreshing. "I won't be a minute," he promised, knowing the best way to handle the situation was to get through it as soon as possible. For him, anyway.

MEG TRIED NOT TO THINK about the fact that Jarett was taking a shower in the next room. She'd considered bolting when he announced his intentions, but it wasn't as if he'd hinted that she should join him, or anything. In fact, he was so casual, it was clear he considered their relationship almost asexual. And it was, she conceded. Strictly business. A service in exchange for money. Jarett needn't know that Meg was hoping to jam a life-time's worth of excitement into one night. Because after this, she'd be back to her simple, slightly boring Peorian existence.

The mirror was irresistible to her—she couldn't stop looking at herself. Nor could she believe that a bottle of hair dye, a pair of contact lenses, skill-ful makeup, and a dress could make such a difference. Kathie would be eating this up. Especially the dress.

And what a dress. Meg turned sideways to study her silhouette. It was exactly the kind of

dress her mother would disapprove of. The kind
of dress that would make men's heads turn. The
kind of dress that had made *Jarett's* head turn.

Meg frowned. More likely, he'd simply been
pleased that she resembled Taylor so closely. She
shot a glance toward the door that led into Taylor's room, and bit into her lower lip.

She really would have liked for Taylor to see
her, to give Meg her blessing. And maybe Taylor
would tell Meg what she wanted her to say, how
she wanted her to act. The actress must really be
ill if she couldn't even talk to anyone, Meg
mused. Or maybe she just didn't want to chance
being seen next to Meg dressed up as herself—
kind of like the Disney World rule about having
no more than one Mickey Mouse seen at any time,
even though there were always several others on
the property. Or maybe it was just embarrassment
on Taylor's part over causing the fire. Meg decided it wasn't her place to judge the woman, who
probably had a million other things on her mind.

True to his word, Jarett was in and out of the
bathroom before Meg had time to work up a good
case of the jitters. He emerged in a cloud of steam
and strong-smelling soap, his hair shiny and
damp, dressed again in solid black—newly
pressed slacks, long-sleeve button-up shirt,
and...socks. He carried a pair of large, low-heeled

black boots by the shank and sat in one of the chairs to shine them with a worn brush.

It was a simple act, shining shoes, but the scene seemed oddly intimate to Meg. She'd never seen Trey shine his shoes, although she suspected he preferred the shoeshine stand at the airport. The muscles in Jarett's arms and shoulders flexed as he moved the brush back and forth in determined strokes. He was a big man, in excess of six feet, and maybe a forty-two across the shoulders. Long arms, large hands, prominent features, including a strong nose. He looked as if he'd come from a robust gene pool, and she wondered idly if Jarett had brothers, or looked like his father and his grandfather.

Unbidden, desire stabbed her, signaling her breasts, which were already sensitized by the uplifting bra. A heaviness settled in her loins, igniting a hum of awareness. Meg's breath caught in her chest—she'd never been so turned on by simply looking at a man. She didn't know how to respond, but she willed her body to quiet.

Jarett tugged on the boots one at a time, then pulled down the legs of his slacks. "Do you need anything before we go?" he asked, without looking up at her.

Could he feel her staring at him, wanting him? Of course a man who looked like Jarett Miller was probably used to that kind of reaction from women. "N-no, I'm ready," she said.

He stood and sighed, then walked over to clasp her shoulders. "Don't be nervous, you look... wonderful."

She couldn't tell him that his touch unnerved her even more than the performance she was about to give. After staring at herself in the mirror long enough, she'd finally decided that she could do this. Everyone would think she was Taylor, and if she ran into any trouble, Jarett would be at her side to intervene. What could go wrong?

"Let's go," she said in Taylor's lilting accent.

He smiled and squeezed her shoulders. "I'll get our coats."

She followed him, stepping carefully in the stiletto-heeled pumps dyed to match the dress. Taylor's foot was the same length, but more narrow, so Meg's toes were already pinched. Tomorrow, she knew, she'd be hurting.

But when Jarett held open a long black cashmere coat for her and looked at her as if he wanted to say something, her heart quickened.

"Is anything wrong?" she asked.

He wet his lips and she knew he was going to kiss her, just like she knew Chip Everett was going to kiss her in the fifth grade by the water fountain. Chip had had glasses, too, though, and the result had been disastrous. As Jarett lowered his head, she realized that this was the first time she'd ever been kissed without her glasses. No maneuvering was required, and she didn't have to worry about her lenses getting steamed up. She closed her eyes and inhaled Jarett's warm breath just before his mouth claimed hers.

It was a hungry kiss, but restrained. His lips were firm and warm, his tongue wet and seeking. The coat served as a barrier to their bodies touching, a safety net. But Meg met him solidly, delving into his mouth with an abandon she'd never exhibited. It was almost as if she was a different person.

Meg's eyes flew open. She *was* a different person—to Jarett, she was Taylor Gee. She pulled away and pressed her lips together, appalled at her lapse. "Why did you do that?" she whispered.

Jarett extracted a white handkerchief from his pocket and wiped his mouth carefully. The stain of Meg's red lipstick stood out in relief against the cloth. "For luck," he murmured, then gave her a casual little smile. "For luck."

Good-luck kisses obviously varied greatly from coast to coast. She conjured up a matching smile. "Oh. Well. Thank you." *Thank you?* She turned to slide her arms inside the luxurious coat, and closed her eyes, trying to block out what had just happened.

Because everything about this man affected her—his look, his touch, his smile. Just being in the same room with him made her feel as if she could spin out of control at any moment. It was…extraordinary, this *thing* between them. At least it was to her. And the night was still young.

She had a fleeting worry that come tomorrow, more than her feet would be hurting.

10

JARETT CHECKED the hallway for strangers before signaling Meg to follow him. "The limo is waiting at the side door," he said, back in bodyguard mode again. He could shoot himself in the foot for kissing Meg back there. Figuratively, he might have done just that.

Despite his growing desire for her, the most foolish thing Jarett could do was to seduce a sweet girl like Meg. He needed her cooperation—now and afterward—to pull off this charade, and he already felt bad enough about not telling her the full truth about Taylor's condition. Besides, it wasn't Meg's fault that he was feeling physically and emotionally deprived by the commitments he'd made. He would not drag her into the mess he was in with Taylor.

Any deeper than he already had.

He tucked his hand under Meg's elbow as they walked onto the elevator. She was shaking. "If anyone speaks to you," he said, "just be friendly. Smile and wave."

"What if someone wants Taylor's autograph?" she asked, her face pale. She had repaired her lipstick.

He patted the breast of his jacket. "I have a stack of autographed pictures for you to give out. Now, when the elevator door opens, we'll exit left and walk straight ahead to the side door where the car will be waiting. I'll be two steps away. Let me get the doors for you, and don't be surprised if photographers pop up."

The elevator doors slid open and a crush of people came into view behind the area roped off and flanked by the hotel security Jarett had arranged. When the crowd spotted her, they began to scream, "Taylor! There's Taylor Gee!" Jarett moved forward, but Meg was frozen in place, her face a mask of apprehension.

"I can't do this," she murmured.

"Yes, you can," he urged. "Remember, you're Taylor Gee. *Smile*."

She swallowed, then took one step forward and emerged from the elevator. Jarett was at her side. The crowd erupted, and cameras flashed like a wave around the lobby. Jarett scanned the crowd, alert for anything or anyone who seemed out of place. Meg did as she was told, walking quickly toward the door, but waving and smiling to the crowd. She pivoted, and played to the cameras, giving them a glimpse of her gown through her open coat. She was something, he acknowledged, floating with a poise that Taylor hadn't yet developed, gracing everyone with a smile that went all the way to her eyes, with the glib honesty of a woman who wasn't concerned about laugh lines.

"Let's see the dress, Taylor!"

She obliged by opening her coat and turning full circle. Catcalls abounded at the sight of her curves, barely contained in the deceptively demure dress, and Jarett was stopped in his tracks by an alien sensation in his chest. Jealousy? Ridiculous. He simply felt protective of Meg for getting her into this.

"Who's the designer?" someone yelled.

Jarett held his breath.

"Kim Cayo," Meg called in a perfect imitation of Taylor's voice. The crowd quieted, seeming to hang on every word. "Kim is a new designer who is donating proceeds from her spring line to the Book in Every Nook Foundation, the cause I'm supporting this evening. Everyone, please take the time to read to a child you know."

Jarett blinked. Although Meg had said exactly what the publicist had sent along with the gown, she'd ad-libbed that last part in a heartfelt tone that sounded like Taylor's voice, but was nothing at all like what Taylor would have said. Unfortunately, Taylor hadn't yet learned about compassion. She'd agreed to attend charity receptions such as this one only because her contract bound her to a certain amount of public service appearances. It was quite ironic for someone whose brother worked in a mission in one of the poorest parts of the world.

"Hey, Taylor!" a man with a microphone shouted. "Would you like to clear the air about the incident at Zago's last week?"

Meg slowed, but Jarett touched her arm. "Ignore them and keep moving."

"Taylor! Did you really flash everyone at the restaurant?" another person shouted.

"What about the rumors that you were on drugs when you took your top off?" someone else called out.

Questions were being fired from every direction, but to Meg's credit, she looked past them, waving and smiling for the cameras.

"Are you a drug addict, Taylor?"

"Taylor, give us a peep now, how about it?"

Jarett shot that guy a warning look, then ushered Meg out the door, past more paparazzi, and into the waiting limo.

He pressed the lock on her door before closing it. Then, fending off the photographers determined to get another shot of her, he circled around back of the limo. He opened the door, slid inside and closed it behind him with practiced ease.

"To the Royale," he told the driver, "but take us the long way." From the look on Meg's face, he needed a few minutes to calm her down. He buzzed up the driver's panel, turned on the cabin lights, and poured them both a glass of wine.

"Oh, no," she protested, but he pressed the glass into her hand anyway. Her red nails clicked against the stem.

"It'll help you relax," he insisted. "Although, you were great back there. Everyone believed you were Taylor."

"Really?"

"Absolutely." She was so lovely, her skin as smooth as a child's, her eyes wide and bright. He had to quell the sudden urge to kiss her again.

She sipped from the glass and winced, then swallowed. It seemed Meg wasn't much of a drinker. Surprise, surprise.

"Did Taylor really do what they said she did?" Meg asked.

He frowned and nodded. "She'd had a little too much to drink."

Meg looked at her glass and he laughed. "Don't worry—I'll stop you before you get that drunk." Unless they were alone. Jarett pushed the dangerous thoughts from his mind.

"I hadn't heard that about her," Meg said, worrying her lip with her straight, white teeth. "Doesn't that make you angry?"

"Sure it does," he said. "She jeopardizes her career every time she pulls a stunt like that."

"No, I mean doesn't it make you angry, considering you're her...you know."

"Her what?"

"Her boyfriend."

He frowned. "Boyfriend? Where did you get that idea?"

Meg shrugged slowly. "The way she looks at you, the way you respond. I can tell you care about her."

Jarett nodded and drank from his glass, then extinguished the light. Things were getting too...personal.

"I'm sorry, I didn't mean to pry."

"No, it's fine," he said, then leaned his head back against the seat. "Taylor's parents took me into their home when I was eleven and she was five. She has a brother who's my age, David. He's my best friend."

"So you and Taylor grew up together."

"Right. I lived with the Gumms until I was eighteen."

"The Gumms?"

He nodded. "Taylor's real name is Taylor Jean Gumm."

"I didn't know that."

He gave a slight grin. "It's not a well-known fact."

She drank from her glass. "When were you in the military?"

He was immediately suspicious. "How did you know I was in the military?"

"From the way you shine your shoes."

He laughed, relieved. Meg really was refreshing. "Guilty. David and I helped out on the family farm for a couple of years after we finished high school, then we joined the Air Force together."

"And how did you...?"

"Hook up with Taylor? After we got out of the service, David and I agreed to accompany Taylor to L.A., since she was hell-bent on breaking into show business."

"Where's David now?"

He told her, skipping the part about how much he missed his best friend.

"And you stayed with Taylor."

He nodded. "I try to look out for her, as much as she'll let me. She's only twenty, you know."

"How old are you?" she asked.

"Twenty-eight. You?"

"Twenty-seven."

"How did you get into the costume business?"

"I didn't—it's my sister's shop. I'm running it for her while she's on her honeymoon."

He made a rueful sound in his throat. "Which makes setting the shop ablaze even worse. I'm so sorry." Although without the fire, Meg might not have agreed to stand in for Taylor, and she wouldn't be here right now. How selfish was that?

"Thanks to you," Meg said, "everything should be repaired and paid for by the time Rebecca returns next Sunday."

He turned his head. "So what do you do for a living?"

"I'm a teacher."

He lifted his head. "You're kidding."

"No. See why I said you didn't have to worry about me telling anyone? I'd probably be fired on the spot if this got out."

His stomach cramped—he should have been more thorough, asked questions. He'd had no idea what was at stake on her side of the equation. "You'd be fired?"

"The school where I teach is very conservative, and lately the administration has been very free with their interpretation of a morality clause in our contract." She lifted her glass toward him. "Impersonating one of the most popular sex kittens in the world would probably be in violation."

"Meg, you don't have to go through with this."

She gave a little laugh. "Yes, I do."

"If you're worried about the money—"

"I know you'd give me the money regardless. But I gave you my word that I'd help Taylor. And you."

Guilt seized him again—he'd taken advantage of her goodness.

"And besides…" She emptied her glass and sighed. "I'm twenty-seven years old, and I've never done anything exciting in my life."

Her admission that she considered this evening an adventure made him feel only marginally better. "Do you even live here?"

"Nope," she said cheerfully—a little too cheerfully, a state he attributed to the wine. "Peoria. I'm just visiting for the week."

He marveled at the amazing series of coincidences that had accumulated for their paths to cross. "What grade do you teach?"

"Second and third."

So he hadn't imagined her connection with that little girl in the shop. "That's why you said what you did about taking the time to read to a kid."

"Yeah. A Book in Every Nook is a great cause."

"Do you have children of your own?"

"No, I'm not married."

He smiled in the dark at her naiveté. In L.A., having children out of wedlock was not only common, it was en vogue. "Ever been married?"

"No. You?"

He laughed. "No."

"What's funny?"

"I'm not the marrying kind." He knew first-hand how elusive the American Dream—husband, wife, and 2.5 kids—could be. Statistics didn't lie. The way to circumvent a broken family, he reasoned, was to not have a family. "I like to travel, I enjoy my freedom."

"Sounds exciting," she said.

But lonely.

She didn't say the words, but he somehow knew she was thinking them. Because he was thinking them too. It made him feel close to her, closer than he'd felt to anyone in a long, long while, and he wanted to hang on to that feeling. He was tempted to tell the driver to skip the Royale, then take teacher Meg Valentine who'd never done anything exciting in her life out for a night on the town. And if the intensity of her kiss was an indication of the passion hidden behind her scholarly glasses, he had a feeling they could find something to do between the hours the clubs closed and dawn.

He looked at her shadowed profile, the angle where she and Taylor differed most. Meg's nose was straighter and her mouth and chin slightly more forward. It gave her a sensual, European look. He had the suspicion that the woman next to him was what his Air Force buddies would call a "sleeper." An unassuming exterior, but unbelievably passionate.

Then Jarett scoffed inwardly. There he went again, projecting his fantasies onto Meg Valentine. He barely knew her. What had compelled him to ask a near stranger to double for Taylor, he didn't know. Or maybe he didn't want to know.

The driver's window buzzed down. "The Royale is up ahead, sir."

"Yes, thank you," Jarett said. As the window buzzed up again, he set aside his half-empty glass of wine. Best to keep his head about him tonight. "Are you ready?"

Meg nodded and smiled, then she put her hand over his and squeezed. Jarett couldn't help himself. He leaned forward and, when she didn't retreat, he gently kissed the wine taste from her lips and lifted his head to look into her eyes.

"Was that for luck?" she whispered, her breath warm and sweet.

"No," he murmured. "That was because I wanted to."

The limo came to a stop, forcing Jarett to collect his thoughts and rein in his libido. If possible, the chaste kiss left him more turned on than the kiss in the hotel room.

He cleared his throat. "Wait until I come around to open the door. Taylor is scheduled to be at the reception for an hour, but we can leave whenever you want."

He hadn't meant for the words to sound like an invitation, but there they were, for her to interpret.

"I'll let you know," she said softly. "Will the press be asking questions?"

"Not after we get through the mob in the lobby. Attendance at the reception is by ticket only."

She suddenly covered her mouth with her hand and gasped.

"What's wrong?" he asked.

"Oh, it's nothing serious," she said. "I just remembered I was supposed to meet a friend here tonight and I forgot to tell him I wouldn't be able to make it." She gave a little laugh. "At least not as the woman he was expecting."

There was that weird sensation in his chest again. "He?"

"A friend of Rebecca's. A deliveryman."

"Was it a date?" Jarett asked casually.

"He's gay," she said. "But he'll be worried if I don't show up."

Stupid relief threaded through him. "When you see the guy, point him out, and I'll give him the message."

"Okay."

"Ready?"

"Ready," Meg said in Taylor's voice.

MEG STEPPED OUT of the car and steadied herself against Jarett's arm. Between the stilettos, the wine and his kisses, she wasn't as sure-footed as she would have liked to have been in front of the throng of reporters, cameramen and cheering fans. She waved and smiled, even though reporters converged on her, throwing out some of the same questions she'd been asked before.

"Taylor, what do you have to say for yourself about the incident at Zago's?"

"Are you an alcoholic?"

"Taylor, is it true that the stunt you pulled at the restaurant has jeopardized your role on *Many Moons?*"

As Jarett directed, she ignored the questions, refusing to make eye contact with the reporters, but the last question gave her pause. *Had* the incident jeopardized Taylor's role on the hit show?

Is that why Jarett had been so adamant that "Taylor" be present at the reception where the president of the network was supposed to make an appearance? Meg maintained her Taylor smile, but her stomach churned. Was she expected to save the day?

A porter started to help her out of her coat, but Jarett stepped behind her and took over. His fingers were warm, curved against her collarbones. Her breasts swelled and budded at his proximity, and a shiver passed over her shoulders.

"Be ready for photos as soon as you turn around," he murmured over her shoulder, his mouth lingering behind her ear a split second longer than necessary. Sure enough, when she turned, the room exploded with flashes.

Drawing on the many times she and Rebecca had played Beauty Queen and walked down a makeshift runway—the coffee table—Meg walked and posed, posed and turned, turned and styled, then waved to the crowd, buoyed by an incredible rush of confidence—she felt sexy and desirable and adored, all at the same time. It was a heady experience.

The crowd cheered and held up We Love Taylor signs. A few fans were even dressed as look-alikes, wearing knockoffs of the yellow dress that Kathie coveted for her collection. Taylor Gee was a very lucky woman, Meg thought as she waved and blew kisses to the fans. People from all walks of life loved her and followed the details of her life. Why would she do something so stupid as to take off her top at a restaurant?

Some shrinks would say because she was an exhibitionist. But Meg wondered if, when Taylor misbehaved so outrageously, she was doing the same thing as precocious little Claire O'Dell when the girl shut herself into the locker of the one boy in class who ignored her?

She glanced over at Jarett, who, true to his word, hovered two steps away, dividing his attention between her and the crowd, his eyes constantly moving. One zealous male fan jumped the barricade and lunged for her, but Jarett pulled him up short and shoved him none-too-gently toward a hotel security guard to dispose of.

Meg flashed Jarett a grateful smile, and, despite the once in a lifetime experience, wished they were on a real date as Jarett and Meg instead of a make-believe assignment as Jarett and Taylor. As if he'd read her mind, he reached out to touch her arm. To an onlooker, it wasn't an unusual gesture between bodyguard and body, she assumed. But it meant the world to her. Every atom in her body gravitated toward him.

Then her gaze dropped to a crest on his sleeve.

A memory chord stirred, and she recalled the picture of Taylor Gee wearing the infamous yellow gown, directing an adoring gaze toward the man cropped out of the photo except for his sleeve and the telltale crest. Jarett.

Taylor was in love with him. And either Jarett wasn't aware of the fact, in that thick, oblivious way men had sometimes, or he was aware of her feelings, but honor-bound to the family to maintain a protective distance. Or maybe Jarett was aware of Taylor's feelings, but thought of the woman as a sister. Meg discarded that option because any man who didn't have the same blood running through his veins would be hard-pressed to look upon Taylor Gee in a sisterly way.

Meg moved across the foyer and entered the ballroom where the reception was in full swing— a band played a jazzy version of "Jimmy Crack Corn" to entertain the dozens of children in attendance. At the happy expressions on their shiny faces, a pang of homesickness struck Meg. She missed her students, missed hearing the little details of their lives that were central to their happiness—their pets, their friends, and their parents, usually in that order.

"Hello, Taylor," a man's voice boomed behind her. She turned to see a handsome man perhaps in his mid-forties, dressed in an impeccable suit.

The man looked like an actor, and Meg's mind raced through the cast on *Many Moons*—was he a character? She glanced around for Jarett, but he had his head together with another hotel security guard. Darn it, she needed help.

"Hello," she said pleasantly, hoping the man would elaborate on his identity.

"I was hoping I could get you alone for a minute or two," the man said in a lowered voice. He touched her arm in a proprietary gesture. "Shall we find a private room?"

One of Taylor's lovers? Regardless, Meg bristled at his presumption, pulling her arm away. "I don't know what you have in mind, but I have no intention of going with you to any room, private or otherwise."

He scowled and opened his mouth, but Jarett suddenly appeared.

"Am I glad to see you—" she said under her breath.

"Taylor," Jarett said, a little too loudly, then turned on a kilowatt smile. "I see you've met your boss, Mr. Heckel."

Meg looked back to the man she'd rebuffed and swallowed hard. He studied her up and down, rocking back on his heels, looking less than pleased. This was the man who held Taylor's future in his hands?

11

JARETT'S HEART THUDDED in his ears as he watched Meg recover, adopting a Taylor-made smile.

"Forgive me, Mr. Heckel, for not recognizing you immediately. This is Jarett Miller, my friend and b-bodyguard."

The men exchanged curt nods.

Meg extended both hands to Heckel, a gesture of grace and friendliness. "It's wonderful to meet you, sir. You're much younger than I expected."

Mort Heckel's face rearranged itself into a less unpleasant expression as he took her hands in his. "I got the feeling, my dear, that you thought I was hitting on you."

Jarett eyed the man warily—considering the way the recently divorced executive was devouring Meg's curves, he probably *had* been hitting on her.

"I'm afraid I overreacted," she said, looking adorably contrite. "I was still upset over a male fan who tried to grab me in the lobby."

Mort Heckel's smile was tight. "Perhaps he heard about your little scene at Zago's last week and assumed you wanted to be grabbed."

Jarett closed his eyes briefly and prepared himself to pull Meg away to safety.

"A terrible lapse in judgment," she murmured. "I'm afraid wine goes straight to my head on an empty stomach, and I'd been dieting. It won't happen again, sir."

Ingenious, Jarett decided. Forthright, apologetic, and with those eyes, impossible not to forgive. Indeed, Heckel seemed taken back.

"I appreciate your honesty, my dear. And I hope you keep your word."

Jarett hoped that *Taylor* kept Meg's word.

"And may I say that the diet must be working. You're even more lovely than your pictures."

Jarett massaged the sudden pain at his breastbone as he watched Meg blush prettily.

The executive coughed, obviously not wanting to go overboard. "You're doing a fine job on *Many Moons,*" he added gruffly. "How do you like it so far?"

"I absolutely love it," Meg said. Then she tucked her hand in his arm. "But right now I'd rather talk about A Book in Every Nook. Shall we go get some punch?"

Jarett hovered behind them, telling himself it

was his job, after all, to stay close to Meg. But deep down, he admitted he was just as interested in eavesdropping on their conversation. A necessity, he told himself, since he might have to intervene.

But, as it turned out, he didn't. Meg Valentine, dressed as Taylor, was in her element talking about the charity and interacting with people. She posed for pictures, and gave away all the autographed headshots Jarett had brought. She removed the gold dangly earrings she wore and donated them to the silent auction. And she surprised everyone by sitting on the floor and reading a classic story to the children gathered round, using animated gestures and different voices for the characters. A toddler scooted close and leaned against her, and he doubted if Meg even realized when she shifted the little girl to her lap.

Jarett stood back, enchanted. It was easy to picture Meg standing in front of her classroom, with a book in the crook of her arm, pushing up her glasses, her braid swishing back and forth. Funny, but even with all the Taylor trappings, when Jarett looked at Meg, he saw nothing but Meg.

"I had no idea she was so charming." Mort Heckel had walked up next to him, his eyes riveted on Meg. Reporters and parents snapped pictures right and left, and Mort was eating up the prospect of good publicity.

"She's a multifaceted woman," Jarett agreed.

"I have plans for her," the man murmured thoughtfully. "As long as she stays out of trouble."

Jarett tucked away the little kernel of information to pass along to Taylor. Maybe it would help balance her reaction when Jarett explained that he'd arranged for Meg to stand in for her. That wasn't a conversation he was looking forward to, but hopefully it would be enough to jar Taylor back to her senses.

A gawky young man with braces caught Jarett's attention. He was some kind of reporter, because he'd been keeping close tabs on Meg all evening, making notes and taking pictures from every angle with a zoom lens. He was probably the president of a local fan club or something.

"Heckel, how's it going?" a middle-aged man holding a cocktail walked up and slapped Mort on the back.

"Carnegie, so glad you could make it."

Jarett stepped back to give the men privacy, glad that the executive had something to distract him from ogling Meg.

Because he wanted to ogle her all by himself.

"Any reason to get out of Peoria, old friend," the man said with a laugh.

Jarett perked up at the sound of Meg's hometown. What were the odds?

"I thought you might be looking for a tax write-off before April," Heckel said.

"You on the board of this foundation?"

"An inherited position from my father," Heckel said with sigh.

Jarett frowned at the floor.

"What are you raising money for?"

"Some library," Heckel said. "Write me a check for a quarter million and I'll make sure you get a plaque over the door."

Carnegie laughed heartily, then stopped abruptly. "I see something that looks better than a plaque. That's Taylor Gee, isn't it?"

Jarett bit down on the inside of his cheek.

"Yeah," Heckel said. "She just might become one of the network's hottest properties."

"She's hot, all right," the older man said.

Jarett shot a glance his way. The man's beady gaze was fixated on Meg and he slowly wet his fleshy lips.

Jarett's stomach turned. Applause broke out, and he was relieved to see Meg had finished the story. He strode to her side to help her to her feet, but another man had beat him to the punch. A slender, black man, handsome and tall. He looked harmless, but then so did most psychopaths.

For a moment, Meg looked as if she knew the man, then blanked her face. "Oh, thank you— sir."

"You're welcome. I'm sorry to bother you, Miss Gee, but I was supposed to meet a friend here. You might remember her—Meg from Anytime Costumes? She said she was going to talk to you tonight. Have you by chance seen her?"

Meg nodded carefully. "As a matter of fact, I did talk to her. Earlier."

"About the fire?" he asked.

"Yes. Everything is taken care of," Meg replied with a languid smile.

"Good. I guess I missed her somehow." The man cleared his throat. "Miss Gee, may I say that I'm a *huge* fan?"

She beamed. "Thank you."

He held out a pen and a cocktail napkin with the name and date of the reception on it. "May I have your autograph?"

Meg hesitated. "I'm sorry, I…can't. Would it be all right if I left something at the costume shop with your friend?"

He nodded. "Sure."

Jarett stepped forward, partly to get her out of the awkward situation, partly because they couldn't afford for the man to recognize her. But the gawky man with braces cut in.

"Taylor, what's this about a fire in a costume shop?"

Meg hesitated, then looked at Jarett.

"Miss Gee isn't taking questions from reporters tonight. Maybe you should move along."

The man's gaze flicked back to Meg. "If you don't mind me saying, Miss Gee, you look different tonight."

Her mouth parted slightly, but she remained silent.

"Have you had plastic surgery?"

Jarett placed his hand on the man's scrawny arm. "I said *move along.*"

The man shrugged off Jarett's hand, but backed away. "*Gee*, Miss Gee, if I were the suspicious type, I might think you were trying to hide something."

Meg didn't say anything. Wearing a smug expression, the man finally turned and walked toward the exit.

"Ignore him," Jarett said near her ear. "He couldn't possibly know."

She turned her smile Jarett's way. His vital signs skipped a reading or two.

"How was I?" she whispered.

"You were…great." He longed to smooth

back the lock of pale hair that had broken free of the twist to rest on her luminous cheek. "Heckel was really impressed."

"You don't think I went overboard?"

"No. You're a big hit." He only hoped that Taylor could live up to the impression that Meg had created. Across the carpeted room, Heckel and the Peoria man headed their way. Jarett clasped her arm and steered her toward the door. "Are you ready to leave?"

"I guess so," Meg said, trotting to keep up.

"Taylor!" Heckel called. "I'd like for you to meet a friend of mine."

MEG STIFLED A GROAN—after a tortuous hour of heightened sexual awareness, watching Jarett circle the room watching her, she was hoping to spend some time alone with him before her limo turned back into a pumpkin. She was playing with fire, she knew, but after tonight, she'd go back to being boring little Meg Valentine. And while the night was young, she didn't want to be reminded that she was just a little cinder girl playing dress up. And she definitely wanted another kiss from her prince.

She smiled as she turned to shmooze Mort Heckel one last time, but the smile froze on her face when she saw his companion. *Trey's father?*

"Taylor," Heckel said, smiling broadly. "Meet Trey Carnegie, Sr. He's a big fan of yours."

Meg was paralyzed, certain that any second the man who passed her the butter at the breakfast table every Sunday would recognize her.

He picked up her hand and massaged it. "Hello, Taylor—may I call you Taylor?"

She nodded, afraid to speak.

Mr. Carnegie looked at Heckel and cleared his throat mildly.

"Taylor, I'll let you visit with Mr. Carnegie while I have a word with your bodyguard—er, Mr. Miller, isn't it?"

Jarett nodded, but he remained rooted, looking to Meg for her agreement. A muscle ticked in his jaw. He was reluctant to leave for her sake, Meg realized, but since she was supposed to be Taylor, she felt obligated to please Mr. Heckel. She nodded almost imperceptibly to Jarett. Mr. Heckel settled his arm around Jarett's shoulder and led him away, talking about something Jarett obviously wasn't listening to.

She tore her gaze from his as he retreated, and fixed her attention on the first button on Mr. Carnegie's suit jacket.

"Can I buy you a drink?" he asked, putting his hand on her waist, pressing her toward the bar.

"Sparkling water, please," she murmured,

careful to mimic Taylor's accent. His hand felt like a cold slab of raw meat.

He scoffed. "Water? That's no fun. We'll have two bourbon and waters," he told the bartender.

She wanted to point out that hard liquor seemed inappropriate for a children's charity reception, but she realized that it would be Meg talking, not Taylor. Choosing the path of least resistance, she accepted the glass with a little smile.

"To new friendships," he said with a lewd glint in his eye, then clinked her glass noisily.

She nodded once, then sipped the drink and forced herself to swallow without twitching. He drank deeply, eyeballing her cleavage. She'd heard rumors of Mr. Carnegie's philandering, but she hadn't believed them. At home with his family, he seemed so devoted. Meg fumed, thinking of sweet Penny Carnegie stuck in that big house in Peoria, probably ironing her husband's socks or something.

"Are you married, Mr. Carnegie?"

He blanched, then frowned. "No. I'm a widower," he said in a pitiable tone.

Meg bit her tongue. "Really? I'm so sorry. How did your wife die?"

He hesitated. "It was a...gardening accident."

"Gardening?" she prodded, enjoying his torment.

"Yes. There was a tiller and a garden hose, and...it was very ugly," he said with a heavy sigh. "I still haven't recovered."

"You must be very lonely," Meg said, dipping a finger in her drink, then touching it to her tongue. She would probably go to hell for this.

But suddenly Mr. Carnegie angled his head. "Have we met before?"

She bit her finger. "*Ow*. N-no, we haven't met before." She conjured up a smile. "I'm sure I would have remembered meeting a man like you."

He squinted, his bushy eyebrows drawing together. "You seem...familiar somehow."

A strangled laughed emerged from her throat. "Well, silly, if you're such a big fan, then you probably watch my show every week, don't you?" She knew for a fact that Mr. Carnegie watched only C-SPAN.

He scratched his temple with his beringed pinkie. "Yeah, that's probably it."

She pretended to drink from the glass and caught Jarett's eye across the room. He looked like a cougar, ready to pounce at any moment. She gave a tiny jerk of her head, and watched Jarett leave Heckel midsentence. Meg turned her attention back to Mr. Carnegie, tolerable now because Jarett was on his way to rescue her.

"I'd like to take you to dinner," Mr. Carnegie said abruptly, then reached down to squeeze her hand with his cold one. His eyes were hooded with lust.

"I'm f-flattered," Meg assured him. "But I'm afraid I'll have to pass this time." Jarett appeared at her side. "You see, I've already made plans," she said, pulling her hand away.

"Are you ready to go, Taylor?" Jarett spoke to her, but he stared down Mr. Carnegie.

"Yes," she said, then flashed the older man a quick smile. "Thank you for the drink, Mr. Carnegie. And thanks for supporting the foundation."

Mr. Carnegie looked between her and Jarett, then turned his back to Jarett. "I'll call you," he told her, reaching up to stroke the hair that tickled her cheek. It was all she could do not to recoil.

"Time to go," Jarett said quietly, although his voice was ominous. Meg gladly walked away from Mr. Carnegie, and was grateful for the comforting touch of Jarett's warm hand at her waist as they threaded their way through the crowd to the coatroom.

"Did you know that Carnegie creep is from Peoria?" he murmured as he held the long black coat open for her.

"Um, yes."

He cleared a path through the shouting reporters in the lobby. "Do you know him?"

Her stomach sunk. "Sort of."

He weaved their way to the waiting limo and held open the door, allowing her to duck inside.

"Who is he?" he asked, crouching to tuck the tail of her coat inside.

Meg swallowed, knowing the fantasy night she'd been dreaming of all evening was not to be. "He's...my fiancé's father."

Jarett straightened as if he'd been hit. The light created a halo behind him, so she couldn't see his face. "Oh," was all he said. Then he stepped back and closed the door.

12

JARETT STOOD ON THE CURB for a few seconds, fighting against the sudden tightness in his chest. Meg was engaged? In love with another man? Perhaps *sleeping* with another man?

It was crazy, he knew, to let the news get to him. No matter how comfortable he felt with Meg, no matter how greatly attracted he was to her, the fact was, he'd known the woman for less than a day. He should just chalk up all his fantasies of taking Meg Valentine to bed and giving her a night to remember, to his relative celibacy over the past year, and let it go.

He had dated occasionally when David lived in L.A., although most of the women he encountered were superficial and brainless. Still, a man had needs, and he enjoyed sex as much as the next man—perhaps more. But after David left, dating had been more trouble than it was worth—bringing a woman back to their apartment would send Taylor into an unbearable funk. And he didn't spend many nights away because he was afraid of the kind of men Taylor might bring home in his absence.

Then she'd landed the role on *Many Moons*. And now that Taylor required his security services, Jarett was suddenly on call at all hours of the day, accompanying her to and from the studio lot, to shoots, and to public appearances. He'd resisted moving into her big new home, but when a stalker had been found sleeping in her guest bedroom, Taylor wouldn't be consoled—and neither would her parents—until he agreed to move into the basement apartment. And even though he had a separate entrance, he'd never felt comfortable asking a woman back to "his place."

Except for the sex, he really didn't miss the dating scene, because he had no intention of settling down. So the news about Meg's engagement shouldn't have bothered him. It had been evident tonight during the storytelling session that she was the type of woman who wanted marriage and kids, which went against the life he had planned for himself. And it wasn't as if he was falling in love with her....

No, he decided as he walked around the back of the limo, he should be grateful. Earlier he'd been worried about bedding her and leaving town, but now he had a good reason to keep his distance and resist the attraction altogether.

He took in a cleansing breath, then exhaled slowly. Yes, everything was as it should be: The marrying kind of people were getting married—Meg and her fiancé, whom he imagined as a rich, soft man who preferred cats to dogs—and the non-marrying kind of people *weren't* getting married. Namely, he and Taylor.

He opened the door and swung inside to sit on the leather seat next to Meg. From his brief glance at her under the illumination of the cab light before he closed the door, she looked pale and tight-lipped. The encounter with her future father-in-law had shaken her up.

Guilt rolled in his stomach—he should never have involved Meg in Taylor's mess. He'd allowed an imagined split-second connection between them to pull him back to her. But in reality, the fantasy he'd built in his mind around Meg Valentine was just as much an illusion as the fantasy men built around Taylor. Both images were idealized, even cliché—sexy and sultry versus innocent and naive. But no man or woman was ever that simple.

Jarett buzzed down the window separating them from the driver and directed him to take them back to the hotel where he and Taylor were staying. There they could deconstruct Meg, and go their separate ways.

"Jarett," Meg murmured. "I'd like to explain."

"No need," he said breezily. "You're engaged—that's not a difficult concept. Congratulations."

"Actually, I'm not engaged...yet."

He looked over at her in the dark. "Yet?"

"Trey asked me to marry him earlier this week, but I haven't given him an answer."

What did that mean? Jarett wondered, even more confused. That she was stringing the poor guy along? That she wasn't happy? That she didn't like her jerk of a future father-in-law? "Whatever," he said.

"You're wondering why I kissed you back," she said.

"Not particularly." *He was dying to know.*

"Well, to be honest, I'm not exactly sure myself. Maybe I felt like a different person made up like Taylor. Maybe I wanted a little slice of her life."

"It's none of my business," he said more brusquely than he'd intended. He was suddenly contrite. Hadn't the woman done him the biggest favor of the century? Pulled off the impossible? And with no small amount of flair?

Her left hand rested on the seat between them. He reached over to cover her hand, swallowing her small fingers with his large ones. "What I meant to say is that you don't have to explain yourself to me. I'm indebted to you for agreeing to stand in for Taylor this evening."

She smiled and turned her hand over so their palms were touching. "Like I said, I thought it would be exciting."

With his thumb, he slowly stroked the fleshy pad of her palm. "I hope you weren't disappointed."

She sighed and closed her fingers around his, entwining their hands. "It was even better than I expected."

They sat like that, holding hands, but sitting carefully apart, even leaning away from each other for several long minutes, until the driver slowed and stopped.

Jarett reluctantly released her hand, then exited to scan the knot of people gathered in front of the hotel. A few had cameras, waiting for Taylor to emerge. One man hefted a television camera to his shoulder. But it was a sloppily overweight guy wearing a ballcap and a long all-weather coat that gave Jarett pause. He waited and watched, but the man simply stood on the periphery with his hands shoved in his coat pockets.

With one eye on the crowd, Jarett opened the limo door and took Meg's hand to help her out.

She smiled at the crowd as she walked toward the revolving door of the hotel entrance. Jarett heard the commotion before he saw it. When he spun around, the man who'd caught his eye was running toward Meg, holding high a large disposable cup. Jarett lunged at the same time the man flung the contents of the cup toward Meg. Something wet hit him in the face as he tackled the guy. Screams rang out.

"Butcher!" the man beneath him yelled. "Tess Canton is a butcher who wears fur!"

Jarett wrestled to subdue the big man, and glanced toward Meg, who stood frozen, her eyes wide. A wide stripe of what looked like red paint started at her cheek, went across her chest, then down the front of her dress.

"Meg, go inside!" he yelled. *"Now!"*

He waited until she disappeared through the revolving door before he boxed the man up the side of the head. "Be still!" Jarett pulled a pair of handcuffs from the hook he wore in a back belt loop, and clasped the man's hands together behind his back.

"Someone call 911 and get the police down here," he said as he pulled the man to his feet.

"Tess Canton is fur-wearing animal butcher," the man snarled.

"I've got news for you, buddy." Jarett shook

him hard. "Tess Canton isn't a real person. And I seriously doubt if the wardrobe budget of *Many Moons* allows for real fur. Get a freaking life."

He left the man in the hands of a hotel security guard who emerged, then pushed his way past on-lookers into the lobby of the hotel. Meg stood to the side, shaking. A couple of coated hotel workers stood near her, offering towels and sympathetic looks.

"Are you okay?" he asked, clasping her arms.

The mole that the makeup artist had so skillfully drawn near her mouth was smeared, and one of her contact lenses was missing. She squinted, her sight obviously impaired, but nodded. At the frightened look in her eyes, he pulled her into his arms.

His heart pounded in his ears as he cupped her head to his shoulder. What if that kook had been brandishing a weapon instead of a cup of red paint? The possible scenarios left him choked with fear, and established just how foolish this entire scheme had been. If Meg had been injured...

He became aware of flashes going off around them.

"Miss Gee," someone yelled. "Are you injured?"

"No, Miss Gee isn't injured," he said, guiding

her toward the elevator and shielding her from the cameras as much as possible. He asked a security guard to get the name of the officer who arrived to place the man under arrest—he would make a statement later.

"Who is Meg?" a male voice asked.

Jarett stopped and spied the gawky guy with braces who had obviously left the reception to come back and wait for them to return to the hotel. "I beg your pardon?"

"Outside just now, you said, 'Meg, go inside.'" The man cocked his head to one side. "Who's Meg?"

Meg had stopped breathing, Jarett realized, waiting for him to answer. "You must be mistaken," Jarett said carefully.

"I don't think so."

Thankfully, the elevator door slid open. "Think what you like," Jarett said. "Right now Miss Gee needs to rest." He guided Meg onto the elevator and turned his back to the door until it closed.

He waited until they were on their way up before tipping up her chin. "Meg, I'm so sorry." He took the towel from her and gently dabbed at the streak of red paint on her face.

"It wasn't your fault," she said, lifting the dangling end of the towel and dabbing at his cheek— he must have been splashed, too.

He was struck by the domesticity of the situation, and a fierce sense of protectiveness swelled in his chest. "I could kill that fur freak with my bare hands."

She gave him a little smile. "I didn't realize your job was so dangerous."

"This isn't amusing," he said. "You could've been hurt."

"But I wasn't," she said matter-of-factly. Then her eyes clouded. "Do you think that reporter suspects I'm not Taylor?"

He scoffed. "He's probably from a tabloid and his headline will be Scientists Clone Taylor Gee, or something stupid like that."

She smiled, and his heart jerked crazily. A smile like that could brighten a person's whole life. The elevator bell rang, announcing the twelfth floor. They stepped apart, and Jarett checked the hallway before allowing her to exit. He didn't breathe easy until they were inside his room with the door closed.

But when he realized they were finally alone, his lung capacity seemed compromised once again.

She shed the coat and went straight to the vanity to wash her face. He flipped on a light in the kitchenette, removed his stained jacket, and wet a paper towel to wipe his face and neck free of the paint spatters. He turned on a lamp in the sitting area, then walked to the far end of the room, past the bed, and pulled the curtains closed.

Just the sound of having Meg nearby, splashing and moving about, made his sex stir, then harden. He looked at the bed and without much effort, he could imagine her lying across the covers, nude and soft and willing. He couldn't remember desiring a woman so intensely, but the entire situation was getting too complicated. She had a boyfriend, after all, and he had no right to muddy the water further, no matter how much he wanted to make love to her. He'd already jeopardized her career and her safety—at least he could leave her relationship untainted.

Assuming that she would have even agreed to come to his bed.

He checked his watch. 10:30 p.m. Jarett sighed and dragged his hand down his face. He needed to do a dozen things—talk to the police, check on Taylor, speak to Rosie, call Taylor's publicist. And all he could think about was Meg.

Meg walked out, drying her face. She wore her glasses and a white hotel robe that swallowed her. "Give me a few minutes to change clothes," she murmured, "and I'll be out of here."

"No," he blurted.

She looked up from the towel. "Hmm?"

He shoved his hand into his hair. "I mean, you should take a shower. If you want to, that is."

She glanced at the door that separated his room from Taylor's. "I don't think so, Jarett," she said quietly. "It's time to end this before we get in any deeper."

Even with the distance between them, her energy drew him. He took a couple of steps toward her. "Are you talking about the body double scheme we pulled off?"

She twisted the towel. "What else would I be talking about?"

His arousal pressed against his fly. He knew he should keep things strictly business between them, but he couldn't. He wanted her—more than he'd ever wanted anything. He wanted her hair falling down and her glasses steamed up. He wanted to give them both a night to remember before they returned to the real world.

He crossed the room in a few strides and stopped in front of her. "Were you talking about this?" He curved his hand around the nape of her neck and pulled her lips up to meet his in a hard, hungry kiss. For a split second, he thought he'd gone too far, that he'd ruined whatever might have been, but then her arms came around his neck, and she opened her mouth to him.

His body leapt in relief and anticipation and

raw desire. He groaned, wrapping his arms tight around her waist. She moaned in response, offering him her tongue, pressing closer to him. Blood pumped through his body, rocketing to his loins. He slid his hands up her back, over her shoulder blades, and into her hair, displacing pins whenever he encountered them. The silky tresses slipped out of their confines and fell down her back.

Restraint, he told himself, *restraint.* Jarett lifted his head and inhaled through clenched teeth, then nuzzled Meg's ear, neck, collarbone. God, she felt so good, smelled so good, tasted so good. He practically shook from wanting her.

"I need to see you." His voice rasped against the swell of her breast.

She suddenly stepped back, her hair wildly mussed, and her glasses askew. Her small hands were splayed against his heaving chest, and she looked as if she might bolt.

Jarett set his jaw to keep from pulling her back to him. He knew how it must look to her—she probably thought he did this sort of thing all the time. But he couldn't very well tell her that she was special, that she was different, because then she might expect something more than a one-night stand. And that was something he couldn't give her.

13

THROUGH THE THIN FABRIC of his shirt, Meg felt the vibration of Jarett's heart beating against her palm. Her own heart was pounding in her chest, whipping adrenaline through her body and short-circuiting her reasoning. There was no future here, only an encounter.

An encounter with a gorgeous, warm man who made her feel fantastically feminine and totally desirable. Hadn't she come to Chicago looking for a few days of excitement? And hadn't Jarett Miller served it up in spades? He wanted to make love to her, and his desire left her weak with wanting, an experience she'd never felt before.

Her inexperience was another cause for concern. Jarett had probably made love to some of the most beautiful, worldly women in the world. What if he found her clumsy?

She looked into his eyes, hooded with longing, and she suddenly realized one truth—they would be remarkable lovers. It was unexplainable, the way their bodies gravitated toward each other, but there it was. Pheromones? Maybe. Magic? Definitely.

Next week she would return to Peoria and, most likely, would agree to marry Trey. They would probably be happy. But she had tonight to be all the things she couldn't be with Trey—daring. Sexy. Naughty.

She looked down, then untied the robe and let it fall from her shoulders. She wore a matching panty and bra set, black and teal, and black thigh-high stockings with garters. The demibra was brief, the panties miniscule. She lifted her gaze slowly. If he laughed, she would crawl back to Peoria.

But he wasn't laughing. His jaw tightened as he scoured her figure head to toe. She drew in her breath, flush with feminine pride, and the tips of her straining breasts popped over the edges of the bra. Jarett inhaled sharply, then stepped closer and tore off his shirt in one motion.

He pulled her against him, rubbing her exposed nipples across the springy dark hair on his chest. The sensation was exquisite, sending shards of desire to the juncture of her thighs. She buried her nose against his collarbone, inhaling the musky male scent of him. He wrapped his arms around her and unhooked the bra, freeing her breasts against him.

She pulled away long enough to discard the bra, and he held her at arm's length. "You're so beautiful, I don't want to stop looking at you."

A rush of self-confidence made her feel bold. Meg wet her lips. "Is that all you're going to do—look?"

He groaned and swooped down for a kiss, then picked her up and strode to the bed. He set her on the edge, then pressed her back, moving on top of her, kneading her breasts before lowering his head to take a swollen tip into his warm mouth.

Meg cried out softly into the darkened room. "Oh, Jarett.... That feels so good."

He laved one nipple, drawing on her breast with incredible intensity, flicking his tongue against the sensitive peak. Incredibly, Meg felt the beginnings of an orgasm humming in her womb. She moaned and drove her fingers into his thick hair, urging him on. He moved from breast to breast, licking and strumming and tweaking until she writhed against him.

She reached down to stroke his thick arousal through his pants, gratified at his groan in response. She pulled at his waistband, frustrated with the cumbersome fingernails. He lifted his head and body long enough to shed his pants and boxers, then rejoined her on the bed.

At the insistence of his erection against her thigh, Meg almost lost her nerve. It was all too…reckless, as if her body had separated from her mind and was rushing headlong into a situation that she might not be able to return from. But she wanted to make him feel just as heady, so she folded her hand around his shaft and squeezed, stroking him up, then down. Moisture oozed against her fingers, and she lubricated the length of him, her body blooming in anticipation of having him fill her.

A long moan escaped him, and he fell against her, kissing her breasts and lightly biting her neck, then her ear. She arched her back and moved her hand in response to his breathless encouragement. "Yes…there…ahhhh."

Then Jarett inhaled sharply and stilled her hand with his. "I'm human," he whispered with a laugh. "And I'm not ready for this to end."

She smiled against his shoulder, happy that she could pleasure him, and surprised to find that she enjoyed hearing him talk to her while they stroked each other.

He moved down her body and she closed her eyes against the longing that pooled in her stomach at his obvious destination. He kissed and caressed his way down to the tiny triangle that covered her mound, then slid his fingers under the fabric and into her slippery folds.

She bucked against the excruciating pleasure and clawed at the covers beneath her. The alien sensations loosened her knees and her tongue. "Jarett...please."

He fumbled with the garters, gasping against her thigh. The sound of ripping fabric rent the air, and suddenly, his mouth was upon her. Meg sank her teeth into her lower lip to stifle a scream of delight. She squirmed against the covers, moving up and back until her shoulders rested against the padded headboard. He followed her, his mouth fastened against the sensitive bead that he now ruled. She swallowed convulsively, gasping for air as her body prepared for an urgent orgasm. The delicious wave flowed, then ebbed, then flowed higher, plunging her over the edge with an intensity that made her open her knees shamelessly, giving him access to all of her.

"Jarett...Jarett...ohhhhh." She pulsed against his tongue, releasing her body's tension. Squeezing his shoulders with her knees, she moaned to the rhythm of her descent from paradise.

He kissed the insides of her knees, then pushed himself up. He was looking for something...a condom she realized with great relief, glad she didn't have to ask. The air was cool against her wet private parts until Jarett returned to lower himself into the cradle of her knees. He kissed her shoulders and her breasts, the head of his warm arousal throbbing against her entrance. Then he moved up to cover her mouth with his, to offer a taste of her own musk to her tongue. As he probed the recesses of her mouth, he moved into her an inch, then retreated, two inches, then retreated. Impatient for him, she clawed at his back, releasing a gratified groan when he rocked his hips and entered her in one long drive.

He gasped into her mouth, gently biting her lower lip. She gripped him with her female muscles, loving the angle her half-sitting position offered. He moved slowly at first, testing her depth and width, and her tolerance for thrusting. She urged him on with her body and her moans, meeting him stroke for stroke. Her legs began to quake as another climax took hold of her, wracking her body with spasms. "Jarett…"

"Meg…"

"…I'm…ahhh…"

"…come…with…me…"

"…ahhhhhh…"

"…ohhhhhh…"

Their bodies collided again and again, then met for one final union. He sank against her, exhaling in satisfaction. Meg was too weak to move, and too satisfied to care. They recovered gradually, their hands fluttering over each other's bodies as their strength returned.

Meg opened her eyes slowly, then straightened her glasses. The weight of Jarett's body on hers seemed nearly as intimate than the act they'd just shared. She stroked his back, pleased that he hadn't rolled away.

Never had she imagined sex could be so thoroughly exhilarating. But swift on the heels of her revelation came the bittersweet realization that they had made love with the abandon of two people who would never see each other again. The sobering thought brought mobility back to her limbs. She nudged herself up, bringing Jarett out of his sensual haze as well.

He grunted, then carefully pulled away from her and sat up, swinging his legs over the side of the bed. "Are you okay?"

"Yes," she whispered, shivering. "But it's getting late."

He hesitated, then murmured his agreement. He stood and walked toward the bathroom, scooping up his clothes along the way. Meg watched his retreating back, marveling over his chiseled, masculine figure. Sudden longing stabbed her—she wanted him again. Already. How brazen was that?

And not very becoming of a woman considering a marriage proposal. She sat up, a stone of remorse in her stomach, and rummaged for her underwear. No, not her underwear—Taylor's underwear. She picked up a strand of hair from her shoulder. Taylor's hair. She held out her hand. Taylor's claws. Jarett hadn't made love to her— he'd made love to a replica of Taylor. The door connecting their rooms mocked her. Taylor was sick, so...

No, Jarett said he wasn't Taylor's boyfriend.

Although he hadn't denied being the woman's lover.

Meg scrambled to her feet and shucked the thigh-high stockings, then strode across the room to retrieve the bag holding her clothes. Trying to ignore her tender areas and sore muscles, she dressed in record time and braided her hair, finishing just as Jarett emerged from the bathroom wearing only his pants. He surveyed her from braid to khaki dress to low-heeled shoes, then scratched his temple. ''I guess you're ready to leave.''

She pushed the end of the braid over her shoulder and straightened. ''Yes.''

He nodded, then retrieved his shirt where it had landed on the back of the club chair and pulled it over his head. She looked away from the expanse of rippling muscle, her skin tingling. He was so confident with his body, a man accustomed to giving and receiving physical pleasure, no doubt. And while she was immensely grateful for his expertise, a small part of her wished their lovemaking could have been as significant to him as it had been to her.

"Something to drink?" he asked, opening the refrigerator.

"No thanks." She just wanted to get the good-byes over with.

He withdrew a bottle of water and opened it on his way to the telephone. After a swig, he turned on a desk lamp and punched a button. "A cab please, at the rear door. Thank you."

The rear door—she'd forgotten she needed to be smuggled out. "Thanks. I'll be going."

"I'm riding with you," he said, sitting in one of the chairs to pull on black socks.

"That's not necessary."

The black boots came next. "Yes, it is."

She didn't argue, but wrapped a scarf around her "see-me" hair and tied the ends under her chin. He pulled another black jacket from his closet to replace the paint-stained one and shrugged into it. Beautifully.

Jarett stopped at the door, with his hand on the knob. He nodded to her scarf, and offered her a slight smile. "Did anyone ever tell you that you look like a schoolteacher?"

She flushed and pushed her glasses higher on her nose. "I *am* a schoolteacher." And with that realization, she plummeted back to earth.

Jarett asked her to wait while he checked the hallway. When he gave her the all-clear sign, she stepped outside, holding the small bag close to her. She watched the door to Jarett's room close, and knew her adventure had ended. No more fancy dresses, no more limousines, no more bodyguards.

Especially seriously sexy ones like Jarett.

They rode down the elevator in silence. Meg's cheeks burned when she remembered the shameless way she'd behaved. Jarett looked tired and shifted foot to foot. Antsy to be rid of her? She pushed up her glasses and felt a little worse.

"We won't be able to discuss our...*arrangement* in front of the cabdriver," he said. "So I want to thank you again for all that you've done for Taylor. And for me."

She conjured up a smile, and nodded briefly, wondering what Taylor would think if she knew just what Meg *had* done for Jarett. Oh, God—what if the woman had heard them from her sickbed in the next room? She winced.

They stopped on the second floor, then took the

back stairs down to the ground floor. A black taxi-cab sat outside the door. As they walked out, Jar-ett's head pivoted side to side, and his hand hov-ered at her waist. An involuntary bodyguard gesture, she realized. Nothing special.

The cab ride was equally as quiet—awkward even. She just wanted to sleep, although she sus-pected she'd have a hard time of it tonight. To-morrow she'd be busy with the cleaners and the repairmen. She sighed.

"Are you okay?" he asked, reaching over and patting her hand.

Like she was a pet or something.

"I'm fine," she assured him.

He whistled under his breath and looked out the window throughout the rest of the ride. When they got to the shop, Meg almost bolted. She'd never been so glad to see anyplace in her life.

"I'll walk you to the door," Jarett said, leaning forward.

"No, don't," she said, gripping the door han-dle. They might draw unwanted attention.

He sat back. "Okay." Then he let out a loud breath. "Well, it's been interesting."

"Yes," she agreed. "Interesting."

He held her gaze and seemed to want to say something. "Goodbye," she said, making it easy for him.

"Goodbye."

She lifted the handle, then opened the door.

"Hey," he said, and she turned around.

"Perhaps our paths will cross again."

She stared at him, her heart thumping. "Perhaps." Then she climbed out of the limo, and walked out of Jarett's life.

The sidewalk was illuminated by tall streetlights. She walked quickly to the shop door and let herself in. The darn bell on the door clanged, scaring the bejeezus out of her. Suddenly, she was exhausted. This was undoubtedly the longest day of her life.

She looked out the window, her heart racing double-time. And undoubtedly the most *memorable* day of her life.

From the cab, Jarett watched with a dry mouth until Meg locked the door, then he signaled the driver to leave.

If he hadn't been so caught up in memorizing the moment he would last see her, he might have noticed the dark car that had quietly parked across the street. And the zoom camera lens protruding from a lowered window.

14

JARETT STARTED AWAKE, instantly on alert at the alien sound invading his subconscious. It took a couple of seconds to orient himself—he'd fallen asleep sitting up, leaning against a headboard, one pillow at his back, one across his midsection. The television was on, but the volume was muted, so that wasn't the source of the sound. His mind raced to fill in the details. Hotel room. Chicago. *Meg.*

The events of the previous evening flooded back, and he conceded a sore muscle or two as he moved to sit on the edge of the bed. The woman had been incredible, both as Taylor and as herself.

A sharp knock shook the door between his room and Taylor's. Ah, now he knew what the noise was. He sighed and stretched, then glanced at the clock—9:15 a.m. It was late for him to be getting up, but he hadn't fallen asleep until around three in the morning. And when he had, he'd been haunted by sparkling green eyes behind unremarkable glasses.

"Jarett," Taylor yelled, still pounding. "Let me in."

She hated it when he locked her out of his room, but he'd been awakened one too many times on roadtrips by a naked Taylor slipping into his bed. His best defense, he'd decided long ago, was a good offense.

He stood and pulled on his pants. The weight of his impending conversation with Taylor sat in his stomach like a stone. Rosie had gladly agreed to keep quiet about Taylor's alter ego until Jarett figured out how to tell her. Last night when he returned from dropping off Meg, both women had been snoring up a storm. He'd hoped that Taylor would at least be well rested this morning, and in a pleasant mood.

He opened the door to her black scowl—apparently "pleasant" had been too optimistic.

"Good morning," he said, running his hand through his hair.

"What the hell is this?" she asked, shoving a Chicago newspaper in his hand.

Taylor Gee Attacked by Animal Rights Activist. And just in case he'd had any fantasies about lying, a full-color picture of him comforting a paint-splattered Meg accompanied the piece.

Jarett sighed—at least he didn't have to think of a way to break the news. "Come in," he said. "I'll make coffee."

Taylor stamped after him, her negligee flying. "I don't want any goddamned coffee. I want to know how it was possible for me to be anywhere with you last night when I don't remember leaving the room! Rosie won't tell me anything. She just stands there shaking like a Chihuahua."

"Sit down, Taylor."

"I—"

"*Sit.*"

She sat.

He put a filter pack in the coffeemaker and ran water into the glass pitcher. "You promised me you'd stop taking the pills."

"What has this got to do—"

"Everything," Jarett cut in, slamming the pitcher down on the counter. Water sloshed over the edge. He inhaled deeply, then slowly let out his breath. "Your pill popping has everything to do with that picture," he said quietly.

"I don't understand."

"Taylor, you were expected to be at that reception last night. Mort Heckel was there—Mac Peterson said he was having doubts about renewing your contract after your little performance at

Zago's. And he's gotten wind of the rumors that you might be hooked on something.''

She swallowed, then tossed her head. ''So?''

''So, Peterson told me to do whatever I had to do to get you there.''

A haughty little laugh emerged from her throat. ''Well, you must have given me a whole handful of uppers because like I said, I don't remember a damn thing.''

''That's because you weren't there.''

She stopped laughing. ''What are you saying?''

''I found a body double to fill in for you.''

Taylor's jaw dropped and she yanked the picture up to her face. ''That's impossible.''

''Apparently not,'' he said dryly, pouring the water into the machine. He flipped the ''on'' switch, then turned back to Taylor.

Her tanned face darkened to scarlet. ''Who is she?''

''Someone local.'' And lovely. And very special.

''How dare you?'' She pushed herself to her feet, and lunged for him. ''This could ruin my *career.*''

He grabbed her wrist before she could slap him. ''No, Taylor, you were well on your way to doing that all on your own. And I should have let you— maybe it would have taught you a lesson.''

She snorted and jerked her hand away. "Surely no one believed it was me."

"Everyone did," he said, then gestured to the picture. "Even you."

Her throat convulsed and her eyes filled with angry tears. "Why do you like hurting me, Jarett? You know I love you."

Jarett sighed and walked to the closet to find a shirt. "Taylor, can't you see? I did this to help you. And it was no easy feat, I can tell you, for either one of us."

Taylor stared at the picture. "Is she an actress? How did you find her?"

He shrugged into a white shirt and buttoned the two middle buttons. "Remember that costume shop you stopped in yesterday?"

She nodded.

"I noticed when we walked in that the girl at the counter was a dead ringer for you."

She scoffed. "That mousy shopgirl? You can't be serious."

He leaned over to tap the picture in the newspaper. "As a heart attack."

Taylor pulled a pack of cigarettes and a lighter out of the pocket in her robe.

"I have a nonsmoking room," he said.

"I don't give a damn," she said, and lit up. When she drew on the cigarette, her eyes bulged.

She crossed her legs at the knee, then pointed at him with the cigarette. "I *thought* there was something going on with you two."

He frowned. "What are you talking about?"

She exhaled the smoke straight into the air. "I saw her flirting with you."

Since Taylor in a jealous rage was not a pretty sight, he was glad he'd taken the time to gather the clothes Meg had been wearing and put them in the bathroom. "You were imagining things."

Her laugh was harsh, and the foot of her crossed leg bounced up and down. "She was totally in awe of you. Did you even have to pay her for the charade?"

"As it turned out," Jarett said, leaning forward to pluck the cigarette from her hand, "you left a cigarette in the dressing room and damn near burned the place down." He stubbed out the cigarette on a stoneware saucer, then crushed the rest of it into the ash. "I paid her twenty thousand dollars, first for the repairs and then to pretend she was you at the reception."

Taylor stared at the cigarette, and had the grace to look contrite. For a full two seconds. "For twenty thousand, I hope she gave a good performance."

"She did. Mort Heckel loved her."

A smile curved her mouth. "You mean he loved *me*."

He nodded. "Yes, he thought she was you, and he was charmed. She apologized for your tawdry behavior at Zago's, and endeared herself to him."

Her eyes narrowed. "Oh, she did, did she?"

"Yes. You should be thanking her, Taylor."

She looked him up and down, then angled her head. "Sounds as if she endeared herself to you, too."

He poured them both a cup of coffee. "Meg Valentine is a grade school teacher from Peoria. She's in town running her sister's shop while she's away. And she's a very nice person."

"How do you know she won't go to the press?"

He set a cup in front of her, then drank from his. "Meg's not like that. Besides, her job could be in jeopardy if anyone found out what she did." He gave her a wry smile. "In case you haven't heard, Taylor Gee isn't exactly a role model."

She stuck out her tongue. "But how did you get her to *really* look like me?"

"Rosie helped—dyed her hair, got colored contact lenses. The makeup artist and hairdresser did the rest."

"They didn't know it wasn't me?"

"Nope. I gave them a picture of you to work from, and when I came back, she was you."

Taylor scowled and dismissed the picture with a wave. "I would never wear my hair like that."

He took another drink of coffee. "Maybe you should sometime. It looked nice."

"That kind of style is for *older* women," she said with disdain. "What is she—thirty?"

"Twenty-seven."

"What's her sign?"

"Huh?"

"You seem to know a lot about this woman."

"Just making conversation, Taylor."

She looked at the headline and her lower lip came out. "Well, this isn't the best publicity I've ever had. And it wasn't even me."

Jarett frowned. "Meg's all right, thanks for asking."

"Was the dress ruined?"

"See for yourself, it's hanging in the bathroom."

Her eyebrow arched. "Oh? She got dressed and undressed in your room—how *nice*."

"Nice and practical," he said, resisting her bait. "Besides, she's engaged." That would satisfy her, even though it had his stomach in knots.

"Engaged?" She looked immensely cheered,

just as he expected. "Well, good for little Meggie."

Jarett marveled at Taylor's transparency.

The phone rang and he walked over to pick up the receiver. Some small part of him hoped it was Meg, although he knew she had no reason to call. "Hello?"

"Jarett, it's Mac. Is Taylor with you?"

"Yeah, we're having a cup of coffee. Come on up." He gave the man the room number, then hung up the phone.

"Who was that?"

"Mac is here."

"Mac Peterson? What's he doing here?"

He looked over the top of his cup. "I'll let him tell you. But if I were you, I'd tell him that last night was your idea."

"Why can't I just let him believe it was me?"

"Because you shouldn't lie to your agent. And I talked to him last night before the reception. He knew you were in bad shape."

Her mouth tightened like a child's, but she fluffed her hair to make herself look more presentable.

When the knock sounded on the door, Jarett let the older man inside, and they shook hands. Mac wore a suit and his traditional English bowler, which he removed and set in the crook of his arm.

"Hello, Taylor," Mac said, his tone expectant.

"Hello, Mac," she said, rising to accept a kiss on the cheek. "To what do I owe this surprise?"

Mac looked at Jarett. Jarett gestured to the table. "Have a seat, Mac. I'll get you a cup of coffee."

Peterson sat in the club chair opposite Taylor and smiled. "Congratulations, my dear."

Jarett made eye contact with Taylor over Mac's head, and shrugged.

"For what?" she asked.

"For whatever it was you said to Mort Heckel last evening. He left a message on my answering service this morning that he wants to extend your contract for *Many Moons* by two years."

She gasped and clapped her hands. "Oh, Jarett, did you hear?"

"I heard," he said, then bit down on the inside of his cheek. "That's great news." He set a cup of coffee in front of Mac.

Mac beamed. "I'll say. I have to admit I was dreadfully worried when Jarett called last evening, Taylor. I'd hate to see you destroy your career over a trifling addiction. If you can stay out of trouble, Mort Heckel will take care of you." He sipped the coffee. "In fact, I think the man has a little crush on you."

Remembering the way the man had looked at Meg last night, Jarett ground his teeth.

Taylor pasted on a tight smile. "He does?"

"I believe so, because he made a comment about how close you and Jarett seemed at the party. I think he was quite jealous."

Taylor shot a look toward Jarett. He knew her well enough to recognize the angry little gleam. "Oh?" she asked lightly.

Mac nodded, seemingly amused. "But I told him that the two of you grew up together, practically brother and sister."

She pushed her cheek out with her tongue, still glaring at Jarett. "That's right. My big brother, Jarett."

"Heckel said you were terrific last night, Taylor. He said you got down on the floor and read stories to the children, and were absolutely brilliant."

Jarett lifted his eyebrow to indicate that she should tell Mac what had really happened.

She stared back defiantly, then turned a charming smile toward Mac. "Let's just say it's a side of myself I don't let everyone see."

"And he said you apologized about the flashing incident, that you acted very mature."

She angled her head adorably. "I thought it was the right thing to do."

Jarett tried not to roll his eyes.

"He thought you were more beautiful in person—prettier even than in pictures or on film."

Uh-oh.

Taylor's mouth tightened and a nerve rash raced up her neck. "Is that so?"

"Yes, the man went on and on about you."

Taylor inhaled deeply, and Jarett covered his cup, fully expecting her to explode any minute. But instead, she exhaled slowly and manufactured a smile. "Good. Then we should be able to get a lot of money out of him."

Mac chortled. "Yes, indeed. Stay close to the phone over the next few days—I have a feeling I'll be calling you with a gem of a deal."

"Unfortunately," Jarett cut in, "Taylor won't be available for a while."

She looked up at him questioningly.

"Why not?" Mac asked.

Jarett pulled a piece of paper out of his wallet. "Because she's agreed to go into a rehab center here in Chicago, and kick this prescription drug thing before it worsens. Right, Taylor?" He gave her a look that said if she resisted, he would tell Mac everything.

She stared up at him, probably wondering whether or not to call his bluff. Then she finally smiled. "Right."

Mac squeezed her arm. "That's wonderful, my dear. You're on hiatus, so it's a perfect time to get back on track. If you play your hand right, Taylor, you're on your way to becoming the next Marilyn."

Her eyes lit up—Jarett knew that Marilyn Monroe was Taylor's idol. "Do you really think so?"

"Absolutely," Mac said, then glanced at his watch. "I have to catch a flight to New York, but I must say, this has been a more pleasant meeting than I'd imagined yesterday." Then he frowned at the paper. "I am sorry that you had to go through that, my dear, but in truth, it happened at a good time. You needed public sympathy, and now you've got it." He patted her hand. "And all because you pulled yourself up by the bootstraps and did what was asked of you."

"Hear, hear," Jarett said, setting down his coffee cup to clap.

Taylor gave him a sarcastic look, but he bounced it right back.

At the door, Mac turned around. "Oh, I almost forgot to tell you." He rummaged in every pocket before withdrawing a pink message slip. "Mort Heckel is speaking at a fund-raiser at a children's hospital this afternoon. He wants you to come by and read a story to the children, like you did last night. I told him you'd be glad to do it."

Jarett passed his hand over his mouth to wipe away the smile.

For a few seconds, Taylor looked as if she might have a cramp, but she recovered nicely and took the note. "I wouldn't miss it."

"Very good," Mac said, then donned his hat. "Cheerio."

Jarett closed the door, then scratched his temple, trying not to laugh.

"It's not funny," Taylor said. "Anyway, how hard can it be to read to a bunch of kids?"

"Meg used lots of gestures. And voices."

She frowned. "You'll have to show me."

He lifted his hands. "I don't know how she did it, she just...did it."

"Well, if Mort Heckel is going to be there, I have to be at least as good as she was!"

He nodded.

She sighed noisily. "I don't suppose the little teacher would agree to teach me?"

He shrugged. "I have no idea." But his heart was already lighter at the prospect of seeing Meg again. "Get dressed. I happen to know she'll be at the shop today trying to repair the damage you caused. It'll give you a chance to apologize and to thank her for what she did for you."

Taylor frowned, then took a drink from her cup. "Okay." But on the way back to her room, she made a detour over to his bed and stooped to pick up something.

Jarett frowned, craning his neck to see what had gotten her attention.

Taylor turned and held up the tiny teal and black panties that Meg had been wearing last night. Worse, the strings that had held them together were mangled little corkscrews where he'd torn them off. Jarett choked on his coffee.

Taylor cocked her head to one side. "Maybe you'd like to thank her for what she did for *you*, Jarett."

15

"HANG ON, SIS," Meg said. Pressing the phone against her side, she carried it into the supply closet so Rebecca wouldn't hear all the construction noise in the background. She closed the door and sat down on a crate of magic wands. "Okay," she said with as much breezy cheer as she could muster. "I'm back."

"Is something wrong?" Rebecca asked.

"No, just noise from the street. I couldn't hear."

"Since the shop is closed today, I wasn't sure you'd be there. Why *aren't* you out doing something fun?"

Meg surveyed her dusty T-shirt, jeans and tennis shoes. "I was just getting ready to go to a movie." If she told Rebecca what had happened, her sister would be worried to death. She'd find out about the fire when she returned home—after the repairs had been made. That would be soon enough.

Rebecca made a rueful sound. "I hate that

you're there all alone. You must be bored to death.''

''No, really, I'm fine.''

Her sister laughed. ''The shop isn't very exciting, is it?''

''Oh…it's exciting enough,'' Meg said, lifting the bandana tied around her head to tuck in a strand of dark blond hair—the color it had evolved to after a dozen washings. ''So what's this about you eloping?''

''Oh, good, you did get my note!''

Meg stared up at Harry, whose permanent grin lifted her spirits—a little. ''Uh-huh. Interesting mode of delivery.''

''Harry is special, Meg, I'm telling you. He'll help you find the right guy. He helped me to find Michael.''

''O-kaaaaay.'' Surely her sister didn't believe that matchmaking malarkey.

Rebecca laughed. ''You probably don't believe in Harry because you've already found your man.''

Meg didn't want to go there.

''How *is* Trey?''

''Trey's fine.''

''You sound funny.''

''Funny, ha ha, or funny, strange?''

"Funny strange. Are you sure everything is okay between you two?"

"As my second graders would say—everything's fine as frog hair. But let's talk about you. Eloping in Las Vegas, Rebecca? Tell me you didn't have an Elvis wedding."

"No, we were married in a perfectly lovely little chapel. It was wonderful."

"Why didn't you tell me?"

"I'm sorry, Meg, but I was afraid you'd try to talk me out of it."

"I probably would have tried, but only because you just broke up with Dickie not that long ago."

"You can say it, Meg—Dickie dumped me. And it was the best thing that ever happened to me. Otherwise, I might have married him and never known what I was missing. Michael is *so* wonderful."

Her sister's tone made Meg wistful, but she was still concerned. "Are you sure he's the one, sis? You two dated for such a short time."

"But I *knew,* Meg. I knew the first time he kissed me that he was the man I'd been waiting for."

Meg swallowed hard—is that why Jarett's kisses had shaken her to the core? Then she rolled her eyes—if Jarett was the man she was waiting for, she'd be waiting a long, long time. *I'm not the marrying kind. I enjoy my freedom.* You had to respect a guy who told you up front that he had no intention of ever making a commitment.

"Have you told Mom that you and Michael are married?"

"I'm calling her next. Wish me luck."

"Okay, but you know how Mom is. Just remember, she means well. We both just want you to be happy."

"Oh, but I *am,* Meg. I am *so* happy."

Rebecca must be since every other word out of her mouth was italicized. "Good. Then congratulations, Mrs. Pierce."

"Thank you, thank you. Now, about Harry—"

"Okay—enough. Surely you don't expect me to believe that this *inner tube* has any kind of matchmaking ability?"

"I know it sounds strange, Meg, but you have to trust me on this. Or if you don't need Harry, you could pass him on to a single friend."

"I'm sure Kathie would get a kick out of him."

"Good, then plan to take Harry back to Peoria with you."

"Okay." She shook her head over Rebecca's fixation with the blow-up doll in the ugly pajamas. "Oh, I met your friend Quincy."

"He's a gem, isn't he?"

"Yeah, he's nice. He gave me a ticket to a fund-raising reception last night."

"Did you go?"

Did she ever. "Yes."

"Did you meet anyone famous?"

"Um...Taylor Gee was there."

"From *Many Moons?* Wow, I love that show."

"Yeah. Oh, I forgot to tell you. She was in the shop yesterday and practically emptied your wall of performance costumes."

Rebecca squealed. "You're kidding? Taylor Gee is wearing *my* costumes—how cool is that?"

"Very cool," Meg agreed.

"I saw on the news this morning that she was attacked last night at some hotel—that was in Chicago?"

"Yeah, right down the road."

"Did you see it happen?"

Meg wet her lips. "As a matter of fact, I did. Pretty scary stuff."

"I guess we'll never know what those peoples' lives are really like."

"I guess not."

"Well, I'd better let you go if you're going to make that movie."

"Oh. Right."

"Listen, there's a chance we might be home a little early."

Meg's eyes widened. "Huh?"

"Just a couple of days early. Don't worry. I won't send you back to Peoria right away," Rebecca laughed. "A company is interested in talking to Michael about franchising the restaurant."

"That's…great," Meg said lightly. "When will you know?"

"I'm not sure, but I'll call you."

Meg's mind raced. The drycleaners would be finished by the time she opened in the morning, but the contractors said they needed until Friday. "Okay," Meg said. "Just keep me posted."

"You're the best, sis. I know the shop is in good hands."

She grimaced. "Right. Have a good time."

Rebecca giggled. "Don't worry."

Meg slowly disconnected the call, then squinted at the handset. Her older sister hadn't giggled since they were kids. Michael Pierce was doing something for her, all right. She just hoped Rebecca hadn't mistaken physical love for romantic love. In the throes of passion, it was easy to imagine yourself in love with the person with whom you were sharing such intense, exquisite, mind-blowing pleasure.

Take Jarett Miller, hypothetically.

Lying in his arms last night, joined intimately, and so…*unbelievably* in tune with each other, her mind had played tricks on her, spinning fantasies about a happily ever after with the man. It was absurd, of course, to think that someone like Jarett would give up his fast-paced lifestyle and carefree bachelor existence to settle for something as tedious as matrimony.

It simply would never happen.

Which was why, she conceded, women like her married men like Trey Carnegie. Men who valued tradition and who, despite their faults, were devoted to preserving their families.

So what if Trey wasn't the most inspired lover, or even that romantic. He was dependable. And maybe he didn't try to catch her eye across a room, but he could always be counted on to contribute to any party conversation. And maybe he didn't cry out her name when he made love to her, but he always made sure her favorite music was playing.

"So, Harry," she said, standing and dusting off the seat of her jeans. "Thanks, anyway, but I don't need your services."

He grinned at her, and Meg shook her head at her sister's nonsense. She was pleased that Rebecca seemed happy, but she would never believe in a million years that a rubber doll had conspired to get her sister and Michael together.

But the doll made her think of Kathie, so she

dialed her friend's number, partly because she wanted to talk to her, and partly because she wasn't ready to call Trey just yet to explain why she hadn't called last night like she'd promised. Kathie answered on the second ring.

"Hello?"

"Kathie, it's Meg."

"Hi! How's Chicago."

"It's...great. How was the swap meet?"

"Disappointing. The best item from *Many Moons* was the bookend that Polly threw at Dean. Supposedly. I didn't buy it."

"Well, you're not going to believe this—Taylor Gee is in Chicago."

"I know, I saw her on the news with red paint all over her."

Meg swallowed. "She came into the shop."

"She did not!"

"She did, and I got you a signed autograph."

"Thank you!" Kathie sighed. "That's the best news I've heard all day."

Meg frowned. "What's the worst?"

"I was at the school yesterday evening for the kids' Science Club meeting, and I heard that Wes Phillips is now being brought up before the school board on morality charges."

"What? Why?"

"Apparently, someone saw him leaving a bachelor party at a strip club."

She frowned. "That sounds pretty harmless."

"They're on a witch hunt, Meg. Three firings in the county yesterday alone. The superintendent is out to make a political name for himself."

Meg closed her eyes briefly. If they knew what she'd done last night, she'd be fired for sure. "You don't have anything to worry about, Kathie."

"It isn't fair. I won't work for a school system that holds its teachers up to some ambiguous ideal, but pays them like paupers."

Meg sighed. "You're right—it affects us all."

"I was hoping you'd say that. Everyone agrees that when you get back, you should be our spokesperson and address the school board on our behalf."

"Me?" Meg croaked.

Kathie laughed. "You are the Teacher of the Year for the entire state of Illinois."

"Right," Meg said, pressing her hand against her forehead. "We'll talk about it when I get back, okay?"

"Sure. I didn't mean to bring you down. Have a good time."

"I will," Meg said weakly. She disconnected the call and leaned against the doorjamb. What was she thinking when she agreed to go along with that stunt last night? Not about her future, obviously.

With a sigh, she opened the supply closet door in time to hear the bell ring on the front door. More contractors? She set down the phone and walked out into the showroom, surveying the demolition of the burned dressing room.

"Hidy-ho," Quincy said, waving from the doorway. He was out of uniform, dressed casually.

"Come on in," she said. "If you don't mind the dust."

He walked in and waved to the guys hefting sledgehammers, then turned a wide smile her way. "I missed you last night, so I thought I'd stop by to check on you."

"Oh. Right," she said, nodding. "I'm sorry I didn't call you—something came up. I went early, then had to leave."

"I know. I talked to Taylor Gee and she told me."

"Oh. Good."

He leaned forward. "Is she gorgeous, or what?"

"Oh, thank you."

"Huh?"

"I mean—" She had to focus. "Thank you...for taking the time to ask about me."

"Oh, sure. You know, she was much nicer than I thought she would be. And she was really good with the kiddos."

Meg nodded. "Good."

"Just goes to show that you can't judge people."

"Right."

He grinned. "And I got a look at that bodacious bodyguard of hers. You're right—I definitely think they're an item."

Meg blinked. "Huh? Why?"

"Because the man couldn't take his eyes off her all night. And I should know, because I couldn't take my eyes off *him* all night." He elbowed her and laughed.

She laughed, then gestured vaguely. "Wait, go back to that first part—you think that her bodyguard has the hots for her?"

"Oh, yeah. Not that every other straight man in the room didn't have a woody for her too, but she saved that gorgeous smile for him."

She swallowed hard. "It was that obvious, huh?"

"Yeah. It kind of surprised me after you said that they seemed mismatched."

"Well, I—"

"If you ask me, they were *gone* over each other."

Meg grinned and bit into her lip. "You think so?"

"Totally. So did she cough up the cash for the repairs?"

"Hmm? Oh, yeah."

"After I met her, I knew she would. Say, she didn't happen to send me anything, did she?"

"Hmm?"

"She said she'd leave an autographed photo here at the store."

"Oh, I forgot."

He frowned. "Forgot to what?"

"Um, I forgot to—" she pointed to the sledge-hammer guys "—thank you for giving me the name of this contractor."

"Sure." He angled his head. "Are you okay?"

"Fine. I'm fine." She let out a loud breath and fanned herself. "Whew—all the dust is getting to me."

He peered closer. "There's something on your face."

"What?"

He lifted a long finger. "It's in your eyebrow. It looks like..." He scratched at her skin lightly, then held up his finger. "Red paint."

"Hmm." She tugged at her T-shirt collar. "It must be from the construction in here."

He turned around, as if expecting to see open buckets of red paint around the shop. She kept tugging.

He turned back toward her. "Hey...did you hear that Taylor Gee was attacked last night when she returned to her hotel?"

"Uh, no, I hadn't...heard."

"It was in the paper this morning," he mused. "Some nut threw—" he looked at his finger "—red paint all over her."

She forced herself to look surprised. "Really?"

"Really."

Quincy pulled back to look at her. "Doing something different with your hair?"

She touched the bandana. "I thought I'd cover it until...later."

He pulled at his chin. "And you've been in the sun, too. You know, Meg, without your glasses—"

The bell on the door rang, and she turned, grateful for the interruption.

She greeted the tall, thin man and explained they were closed. He looked vaguely familiar.

"Meg Valentine?" he asked.

"Yes. Who are you?"

"Phil Shotz from the *Tribune*."

"Can I help you?"

"Are you the same Meg Valentine who was just named Teacher of the Year?"

She swallowed. "Y-yes."

He smiled, revealing braces, and she suddenly recognized him as the nosy reporter from the previous night. Panic bolted through her.

"I'd like to talk to you about Taylor Gee."

16

MEG'S STOMACH DROPPED. She glanced to Quincy, then back to the man, trying to remain calm. "I'm sorry, the shop is closed. If you'd like to talk about my award, you'll have to arrange it through the school where I teach. That's all I can help you with."

Quincy straightened and leveled his gaze at the man. "In other words, I think you need to leave."

The man looked past him and smiled. "Miss Valentine, I know what happened last night. I followed you, and I have the photos to prove it."

She had to fight to keep her knees from buckling. "I d-don't know what you're talking about."

He held up a business card. "Yes, you do. If you want the photos and the negatives, my fee is on the back. Call me by the end of the day. Otherwise, they're going to be plastered all over the Internet." He turned and left the shop.

Meg's throat convulsed, and she sank against the counter, blinking back tears. Her life was over.

Quincy was immediately by her side. "Was he talking about what I think he was talking about?"

She closed her eyes and nodded.

"That was *you* last night?"

"Can you believe it?"

"Well, you look like her, but…no, I can't believe it."

"It's a long story," Meg said, "but basically I'm in a lot of trouble. If my school board finds out that I dressed up like a sex kitten…" She groaned. "Quincy, can you stay here with the contractors? I need to go see someone."

"Sure. Take as long as you need."

She needed to see Jarett, assuming he and Taylor were still in town. She hadn't even asked him how long he was staying. But if Taylor was still sick… She hated to wish the other woman ill, but if they'd left town, she was a goner.

She grabbed her purse and the business card the man left, then hailed a taxi, dirty clothes and all. At the hotel, she used the back stairs. When she stepped up to the door, her heart was pounding like mad. She knocked on Jarett's door, and a few minutes later, to her surprise, Taylor answered.

"We're not ready for the room to be cleaned," she said.

"I'm Meg Valentine," she said. "You probably don't remember me—"

"From the costume shop, right?" Taylor looked her up and down.

"Yes."

She laughed. "So you're my little body double."

"Y-yes. I see you're feeling better."

She narrowed her eyes. "I don't care what Jarett told you, I'm not an addict."

Meg blinked. "He said you had allergies."

"Oh." She pursed her mouth. "That's right."

"Is Jarett here?"

She smiled. "He's in the shower."

Her implication couldn't have been more clear, but Meg didn't have time to think about her stupid lapse of judgment. "I need to talk to him."

"What about?"

Meg looked around the hallway. "May I come in?"

Taylor considered her for a minute, then waved her inside. "Let's go to my room."

Meg walked in, her heart jumping in her chest at the poignantly familiar surroundings. "I have a problem."

"Oh?"

Taylor led her through Jarett's room and to the connecting door, which wasn't locked. She couldn't help but notice the bed was mussed, and she wondered if they had—

Meg forced her mind back to the matter at hand. Taylor closed the connecting door and strangely, locked it. "And just what is your problem?"

She held out the card the man had given her. Her hand shook violently. "He's a reporter, and he came to my shop this morning. He said he had followed us last night and he had pictures."

"That prove you were standing in for me?"

"He didn't show me the pictures, but I assume so."

Taylor lit a cigarette. "How much does he want?"

Meg pointed to the back of the card.

She turned it over. "Ten thousand dollars. Why wouldn't he bring the photos to me?" Taylor asked. "I have more money."

"I guess he knew where to find me, and assumed I would come to you. I don't have that kind of money, Miss Gee."

"Or you're in on it with him," Taylor said.

Meg pushed her glasses higher. "What?"

Taylor looked at her with venom in her eyes. "And I really don't care if you are. Here's my deal." She took another drag from her cigarette.

"I'll keep this card and pay the little creep what he wants. And you will stay away from Jarett."

She swallowed and shook her head. "Stay away?"

"We're going to be in town for a few days," Taylor said, exhaling smoke in Meg's face. "And I want to make sure *you* are not going to be *my* problem."

Meg didn't know what to say.

Taylor gave a little laugh. "Good God, you're in love with him, aren't you?"

"No."

"Of course you are. Well, let me tell you something. Jarett is mine. He loves me, but he's afraid my parents will object if we marry." She smiled. "Don't you see? He only slept with you because you looked like me."

Meg's heart squeezed, but she refused to cry in front of this woman. "I can't believe I tried to help you," she whispered.

"You're not fooling me, sister. You did this to get to Jarett."

"No, I didn't."

"Well, I'm in control now," she said. "Jarett and I are coming to your shop today to see you, and you will pretend this conversation never happened."

She swallowed and nodded.

"And if Jarett tries to see you again, you'll tell him you're not interested."

She swallowed and nodded again.

"Now get out."

Meg jumped, then backed away, toward the door leading to the hallway. She just wanted to get away from these horrible people.

Taylor followed her. "Remember, if Jarett comes sniffing around, *just say no.*"

Meg stumbled into the hallway and ran for the steps. Her tears were falling freely now. How stupid could she have been? Taylor hadn't been ill last night, she'd overdosed on something. Jarett had lied to make her feel sorry for the woman. He'd gone to great lengths to cover for his lover, that's for sure.

Well, Taylor didn't have to worry—if Jarett Miller ever came "sniffing" around again, she wouldn't have to make up an excuse to stay away from him.

JARETT STEPPED OUT of the shower, his ear cocked to the door as he dried his back. His mind must be playing tricks on him—he could have sworn he heard Meg's voice. He slipped into a robe, tied the sash, and stepped out into the room.

Taylor lounged on his bed in a skimpy gown. "Did I hear someone else just now?"

She pursed her mouth and shook her head. "No. It must have been the television."

He frowned. "Don't you have your own room and your own television?"

She sighed. "I'm lonely."

"Well, go get showered and dressed, and we'll go out. Don't forget about the storytelling session."

A frown marred her pretty face. "How could I?"

"Don't worry, Meg will help you," he said with a grin. Then he walked back to the bathroom, whistling under his breath. He couldn't wait to see her again.

17

MEG'S EYES STUNG, but she'd convinced herself
it was from all the sweeping she'd done. She
stopped and used the tail of her T-shirt to dab at
the moisture in her eyes, then resumed cleaning
up. The contractors had left for the day, and she'd
finally convinced Quincy that everything was fine.
She stooped to fill a dustpan, then walked into the
supply room closet to fetch another trash bag.

Inside the closet, a cracked mirror leaned
against the wall. At the sight of herself, Meg came
up short. Talk about Cinderella—covered in white
ash, hair bound in a kerchief, clinging to a broom-
stick. She bore no resemblance whatsoever to the
sexy siren she'd been last night. Funny, though,
she was still the same person.

Meg sank to the crate, rested her head on her
knees and gave in to tears. Her stomach ached,
and her throat felt raw from holding back emotion
since she'd returned from the hotel. She felt sad
and stupid and sorry for herself—sorry that she

hadn't realized until this afternoon how good her life really was.

She loved teaching, she loved the light of understanding on a child's face, she loved knowing that she was making a difference in the world, even if she only had an impact on one child, and even if she never knew about it. And she loved that darn bell that maintained order in her day.

How stupid to think that she could embark on some wild adventure that went completely against her nature, and not have it affect all the things she'd built over the years—her teaching career, her solid reputation, her relationship with Trey. One foolish hour of passion with Jarett, and she'd been ready to toss Trey aside at the slimmest possibility that Jarett might want to see her again.

Passion was a powerful emotion, making an ordinarily sane individual do and feel absurd things. It skewed a person's outlook, messed with priorities, and caused general chaos. Her only consolation was that no matter what *his* motives were, she had slept with Jarett because she'd truly felt a connection with him. Perhaps he'd robbed her of her pride, but no one could take away the new sense of self-awareness that the experience had given her. Still, the price had been high.

She sniffed mightily against her knee, reminding herself to be at least grateful that the wretched reporter would be paid to go away. And if Rebecca came home early, Meg could get back to Peoria soon and try to put this mess behind her.

Meg lifted her head and looked at Harry. "Okay, now what?" she asked, wiping her eyes. "You got me—I'm so desperate that I'm willing to talk to *you*." He grinned stupidly down at her, and she finally smiled.

"Rebecca thinks you have magic *love* powers," she said, wiggling her fingers in his direction. He grinned.

She sighed. "Okay, if you've got some kind of love vibe, lay it on me." She stood and threw open her arms. "Did you hear me? I'm open to having a man in my life, and I'd appreciate any guidance you can give me."

The bell on the door tinkled, and Meg hiccupped in surprise. She took another swipe at her eyes, then emerged from the supply closet, her heart pounding.

Two men stood in the showroom, their backs to her. When they turned toward the sound of her footsteps, she stopped, shocked. "Trey, Mr. Carnegie."

"Hi." Trey smiled and held out his arms, and she thought how endearing his face was. He was a tall, slender man, with thinning sandy-colored hair and grayish eyes. She stopped short of embracing him, clasping his hands instead, saying she didn't want to pass along some of the dust she was wearing. "I'm a mess," she told him apologetically, before turning and greeting Trey Carnegie, Sr.

"Hello, Mr. Carnegie." She tried to push away her memories of her unpleasant encounter with him the previous evening, but she was having a hard time.

"Hello, Meggie."

She hated that silly pet name.

He tweaked her nose. "And I'm hoping that very soon, you'll call me 'Dad'?"

She avoided his question by looking back to Trey. "What a surprise. What brings you to Chicago?"

"Father was here for business. I knew you were here, and when I didn't hear from you last night, I thought what the heck—I'd just fly up and say hello." Even if she married Trey, she'd probably never get used to the idea of having a family jet at her disposal.

A flush warmed her cheeks. "I'm sorry I didn't call last night. I was…delayed."

He waved off her concern. "I figured you were out with friends."

She nodded.

"What happened here?" Mr. Carnegie asked,

gesturing toward the pile of demolished rubble that she hoped to have cleared by the time the contractors returned in the morning.

"There was a little fire," she said.

Trey's face creased with concern.

"But no one was injured," she added. "But there was some damage to a dressing room. And the smoke got into everything."

"What a relief," Trey said, his concern for her obvious on his face.

"Some of these costumes are a little risqué, aren't they?" Mr. Carnegie asked, disapproval clear in his voice.

Meg bit her tongue, not believing the man's nerve. Last night he'd told Taylor, the woman he was hitting on, that his wife was dead. And now he was on moral patrol?

Much like the Superintendent and school board, she thought grimly.

"Guess where we've been?" Trey asked with a smile.

"At our jeweler's," his father blurted. "Getting you a proper ring."

She looked back to Trey. "But I thought you said—"

"I know I said you could pick it out, and you can." He slipped a ring box from his pocket. "If you don't like this one, you can take it back and get one that you do like. But at least you'll have a ring for now.''

''But Trey—''

''Just look at it,'' he urged, pressing the box into her hand.

He had such a hopeful expression, she couldn't bear to disappoint him. She opened the ring box and gasped. Emerald-cut solitaire in a platinum setting—what was not to like?

''What do you think?'' he asked.

''It's…extraordinary,'' she murmured. How many women would trade places with her at this moment?

''I had it sized,'' he added shyly.

''Try it on,'' his father boomed, less tactful.

She withdrew the ring and slipped it on her left ring finger. The simple pearl ring her mother had given her for graduation was the only jewelry she wore regularly, so the weight of this bauble would take some getting used to.

''It's perfect,'' she said, holding it up to the light. Dazzling prisms danced off the surface. At the sound of the bell on the door, they all turned.

Meg's stomach pitched at the sight of Jarett holding the door open for Taylor. A gleam of feminine challenge lit Taylor's pointed gaze. But the woman needn't have bothered giving Meg the evil eye. Meg knew what was expected of her.

18

SINCE JARETT ONLY HAD eyes for Meg, he didn't immediately realize that she had visitors, or who they were. He noticed the older man first, only because he looked familiar… He'd attended the reception last night, the man he'd practically had to peel away from Meg. Her future father-in-law.

Meaning the other man was her fiancé? His gaze went immediately to the younger man, who appeared to be hovering around Meg's hand.

"Oh, let me see," Taylor said, bustling into the middle. "Meggie, it's a lovely, lovely ring." She smiled at the couple. "Congratulations."

Jarett's chest suddenly felt as if it were bound. Meg had warned him, hadn't she? Yet it just didn't feel right, his Meg getting married to another man. Only last night she'd cried out *his* name in climax. Frustration rolled through him, especially since she appeared to be avoiding eye contact with him.

"You're Taylor Gee," Meg's fiancé said, staring.

Imbecile—didn't he know that Meg was more beautiful, inside and out?

Taylor beamed. "Yes. And you are?"

"Trey Carnegie, Jr."

"My...fiancé," Meg said. "And this is Trey's father, Trey Carnegie, Sr."

"We met last night," the older man told Taylor.

"We did?" Taylor looked to Meg, who returned an almost imperceptible nod. "Of *course* we did. So good to see you again." Finally she looked back to Jarett. "Gentlemen, meet my dearest friend and my security guard, Jarett Miller."

Jarett stepped forward and shook their hands, both of which were a bit too soft for his tastes. But the younger Carnegie seemed cordial enough.

"How do you know each other?" Mr. Carnegie, Sr. asked Meg.

Meg looked at Taylor, and Taylor adopted a charming expression. "We met when I came in shopping yesterday. We became quite well acquainted, didn't we, Meggie?"

Meg nodded, but seemed fidgety. "What can I help you with today, Miss Gee?"

Taylor looked back and forth between the Carnegies. "It's a personal matter, boys, do you mind?"

"How about if we come back to take you to

dinner, sweetie?'' This comment was from Jr. to Meg.

Sweetie?

She nodded. ''Around eight?''

Meanwhile, Carnegie, Sr., couldn't get a good enough look at Taylor's chest. ''Are you available to join us, Miss Gee?''

''No,'' Jarett and Meg said at the same time.

Jarett tried to paste on a pleasant smile. ''Remember the children's hospital visit, Taylor.''

''Oh, that's right,'' she said, looking sorrowful. ''Maybe another time.''

''Absolutely,'' Carnegie, Sr. said, his gaze adoring. The men moved closer to Jarett, out of earshot of the women. ''Son,'' the older man said to him. ''You have to have one of the best jobs in the world, looking at *that* all day.''

The younger Carnegie might have shared his father's sentiments, but he remained silent, which Jarett respected. Still he couldn't resist asking a few questions. He turned to Trey.

''What do you do, Carnegie?''

The younger man shrugged. ''Family business.''

''Petroleum, real estate, transportation,'' Carnegie, Sr. said loudly. ''If it's making money right now, Carnegie Enterprises is invested in it.''

He nodded. They were filthy rich. ''Say, I'm

looking for a place to buy a show dog," he said to Meg's fiancé. "Can you recommend a good breeder?"

Trey shook his head. "I have a cat, myself."

"Ah. Well, thanks anyway."

Jarett watched his retreating back, wondering how he and Meg had met, the kinds of things they did on dates, and if they lived together.

"Are you two planning to have children?" Taylor asked Meg.

Meg looked at her strangely. "We're not even married yet."

But of course she would have children, Jarett thought. Meg probably wouldn't feel complete if her house wasn't as noisy as her classroom. He swallowed hard. Good for them—they made a nice couple. They would have beautiful daughters and tall sons.

"I didn't congratulate you," he said, walking closer.

She didn't look up.

"So, congratulations."

She flitted her gaze over him, and nodded. "Thank you."

"Meg," Taylor said suddenly. "Jarett explained what a wonderful job you did filling in for me last night, and I wanted to personally thank you."

"You're welcome," Meg murmured.

Taylor gestured to the pile of debris that used to be the dressing room. "He also explained that one of my cigarettes caused some minor damage?"

Jarett loved how she used passive tense, as if to put the blame on the cigarette rather than herself.

Meg nodded. "Yes, but—"

"I'm so, so sorry for the inconvenience," Taylor said, sympathetically. "I understand that Jarett already arranged for compensation?"

Meg nodded woodenly. "Yes."

Jarett frowned. Although he tried not to judge Taylor too harshly—after all, she did say thank you and make apologies, just as he'd directed. But her delivery could use some polish.

"Meg," he said.

He'd managed to catch her unaware. She looked up, her eyes wide and luminous behind the glasses before she looked away. "Yes?"

"Taylor knows she doesn't really have the right to ask, but she needs a favor."

"What?"

Taylor frowned in his direction, then looked back to Meg. "Mort Heckel liked whatever it was you did with the kids last night. You know, reading. Can you teach me how to do it?"

Meg pushed up her glasses. "You want me to teach you how to read?"

Jarett smiled—it was the first show of spunk Meg had shown since they'd arrived.

"No," Taylor snapped. "I want you to teach me how to read aloud to kids."

"How to tell stories," Jarett added. "If that's possible. And if you have time."

"Why?" she asked Taylor.

Taylor sighed. "Because Mort expects me at a children's hospital in a few hours and wants me to do what you did last night."

The first real smile since they'd arrived curved Meg's lips. "Really?"

"Really," Taylor said flatly. "So I need to know your tricks."

"If you have time," Jarett added.

"Right," Taylor said.

Meg looked dubious. "I guess I can give you a few pointers."

"Great," Taylor said quickly. "Let's get on with it."

"Do you know what book you'll be reading?"

Taylor blanched. "Is that important?"

Meg rummaged behind the counter until she came up with paper and pen. She hesitated a moment, lost in thought, then began to write on the paper. "Here are a few titles to pick up at the bookstore. You might get a few extra copies to leave with the kids.''

"Write that down," Taylor said.

"Now," Meg said. "When you read, use a stage voice, really enunciate and project. *How now Brown cow,*" she said loudly, then looked to Taylor. "You try it."

Jarett leaned back against a column and watched Meg teach. She was in her element, and he'd never been more attracted to her. He knew what lay beneath those dusty garments—the layer of ash just made him want to make love to her in a shower. He'd bet Jr. had never taken her in the shower.

He shook himself mentally, and simply observed the situation. Meg explained to Taylor about making eye contact with the audience, how to make big gestures, and a few common stage noises. The odd thing was, Taylor seemed to be paying attention.

"This is like putting on a one-person play," Taylor said at one point.

"Exactly," Meg said, before going into the finer points of character voices.

Side by side, Meg and Taylor were so different, he could scarcely remember that Meg had looked so much like his charge just last night, that other people couldn't see the glaring differences. His sex hardened just watching Meg move. She was graceful, like a dancer. It was her natural body control, he realized suddenly, that made her such a wonderfully responsive lover.

He'd spent most of the day investigating the center that Taylor had agreed to enter for two weeks of rehab. So far, so good—it seemed to be a discreet facility. But his research had taken twice as long because he simply couldn't stop thinking about Meg in his bed, under the influence of his hands, his tongue, his body. He hadn't slept with a huge number of women in his life, but he was no monk, either. And to date, none of the experiences had warranted more than a vague sense of gratitude on his part.

So what was different about Meg Valentine? Why did the woman stick in his mind like a burr?

"So that's it?" Taylor asked.

"Well, it helps if you like kids," Meg said.

Taylor bristled. "I like kids."

"You hate kids," Jarett reminded her.

Taylor frowned. "I can pretend to like kids for a couple of hours."

He was embarrassed for her, Jarett decided, shaking his head.

"Kids pick up on that kind of thing," Meg said quietly, her face serious. "Remember, some of these kids are never going home. Others are in pain every minute of every day. I don't think it's too much to ask to put one of them in your lap if they want to get close." Meg pushed up her glasses and averted her gaze.

Even Taylor had the decency to look remorseful. "I'll do my best," she said in a tone so normal, he almost didn't recognize it.

"Taylor, could I have a private word with Meg?"

Taylor pulled herself up. "I don't see why not. I need to go to the ladies' room before we leave anyway." Meg pointed the way, and by mutual consent, neither she nor Jarett said anything until Taylor had left the room.

He claimed the wooden stool that Taylor had vacated. Meg sat with her hands wrapped around her knees, waiting.

"Meg, I'd like to see you again."

She turned her head abruptly. "That's impossible."

"Why?"

She lifted her hand. "Because I'm engaged to another man. Last night was a mistake, Jarett."

"Then why did you do it?"

She shrugged. "Last fling before I settled down?"

Her glib answer cut through him.

"There's something between us here, don't you feel it?"

She made an exasperated sound. "Yes—lust. Jarett, you told me you're not interested in being tied into a relationship. Well, guess what? I'm not interested in having a purely sexual one. I know it probably seems backward to you, but I like the idea of having security in my life, of knowing someone is going to be there for me. That that person needs me as much as I need him."

"And that person is Carnegie?"

She looked away. "Yes."

"The way it was between us last night—is it like that with him?"

She hesitated for so long, he already knew her answer. She finally lifted her gaze. "No, it's never been like that between me and Trey. But he loves me, and he would never hurt me." She choked. "He doesn't deserve the way I betrayed his trust."

"You don't strike me as the kind of person who would betray his trust lightly."

"Really?" she asked, then laughed. "Do you know I've been told that my entire life? That I seem like the kind of person who would do this, or not do that? Well, I have a news bulletin for you, and for everyone else." She swallowed. "I did betray his trust lightly, all because I wanted a one-night stand with a great-looking guy.''

He hadn't expected it to hurt so much—he really thought their encounter had meant something to her. Because it had to him.

She climbed down from the stool. ''Don't try to put me on a pedestal—I don't want to be up there.''

He stood and clasped her arm as she turn to walk away.

''Meg, do you love this guy? If you do, tell me and I'll walk away.''

She turned back to him, her eyes bright. ''You know something, Jarett? You're going to walk away no matter what I say—that's how you're wired. But yes, I do happen to love him. Goodbye.''

He watched as she disappeared through a set of swinging doors into another part of the building. It took everything in him not to go after her. But she was right—he wasn't prepared to offer her the kind of stability, the kind of future that Carnegie offered? They'd known each other for mere hours—he couldn't very well expect her to turn her back on Carnegie because the sex had been spectacular.

Taylor emerged looking very pleased with herself. "Are you ready?" she asked, giving him a sweet smile.

"Yeah, I'm ready," he said, heading for the door. "There's nothing for me here."

———————

19

MEG SURVEYED the restored dressing room with satisfaction, then inhaled deeply—not a trace of smoke. The costumes were freshly cleaned, and the commercial cleaners had used a citrusy detergent on the floors and walls. Very nice.

Just in time for Rebecca to arrive home, two days early as she'd predicted. Meg was planning to stay long enough to have dinner with her sister and new brother-in-law, then she'd be back in Peoria by ten o'clock or so. She preferred driving in the daylight, but at this point, she just wanted to leave Chicago. Her bags were already packed and in the car.

There were too many bad memories here.

Besides, she was exhausted. Every night she lay down, tired and aching, and every night she tossed and turned, replaying scenes with Jarett in her mind over and over and over. His lovemaking was so ingrained in her memory now, she suspected she'd be babbling about it in her old age when all of her other memories had faded.

She snapped her fingers, suddenly remembering that she had another item to pack. She opened the supply room closet and stared at Harry, the blow-up doll with something extra, according to her sister. And hadn't Trey shown up just after she told Harry to work his magic on her?

Meg angled her head. "Okay, maybe you're not magic, but you do kind of grow on a person."

He grinned at her, and she laughed. "How many strange looks do you think I'll get on the Interstate with you sitting in the passenger seat?"

She moved a crate and a chair to clear a path to him. Might as well wrestle him out and size up his traveling requirements.

The bell on the door rang. "Hidy-ho!"

"I'm in the closet, Quincy!"

He appeared a few seconds later and looked over her shoulder. "Hey, Harry."

Meg shook her head. "It's crazy, but you almost expect him to answer."

"Are you putting him on display?"

She laughed and pointed to Harry's ever-ready arousal. "I don't think that would be a good idea. I'm taking him back home to a friend of mine."

"A single friend?"

"Yes," she said dryly. "Not that I believe any of that malarkey about a good luck love charm."

"Hey, you're engaged, aren't you?"

She looked at her ring and nodded. "But Trey asked me to marry him before I came to Chicago."

"Well, maybe Harry helped you make up your mind."

"Okay, I give up. Just help me get him through the door, okay?"

"Sure thing."

She picked up the doll by his arms and pushed him through the doorway. Quincy helped with wayward limbs and baggy pajamas. When Harry was out, Meg turned around to rearrange items in the spot he'd taken up, and gasped.

"What is it?"

A bulky envelope lay in the floor. "It's the missing deposit." Her heart thudded as she retrieved it, and her hands shook.

"That's great!" he said, clasping her shoulder.

But her stomach had fallen. "No, it's awful."

He frowned. "How is finding fifteen thousand in cash awful?"

She clamped her hand to her forehead. "Don't you see, Quince? If I hadn't lost this cash, I would never have accepted Jarett's deal to impersonate Taylor. I only did it to make myself feel better about the money he gave me to cover the deposit." She thought she was going to be sick.

"How did the deposit get in here?"

Meg closed her eyes, trying to remember the details. "I came in to get a night deposit bag, and I guess I had the envelope with me. That's when the fire broke out, and I ran for the fire extinguisher."

"But I thought the firemen found the night deposit bag in the dressing room."

"They did, but I must not have had time to put the envelope in the bag. I guess I dropped the envelope in here, and the night deposit bag when I was using the extinguisher in the dressing room."

"So all this time, Harry's been standing on fifteen grand?"

Meg sighed and managed a little laugh. "I suppose you're right."

A slow smile crept up Quincy's face. "So what you're saying is that if it hadn't been for Harry, you would never had spent the evening with Jarett Miller."

She scoffed. "That's not what I'm saying at all." Then she squinted. "Wait a minute—that is what I'm saying."

Quincy's low chuckle rumbled out. "I wouldn't have believed it, if I hadn't seen it first-hand."

"But what am I going to do · with all this

money? I used the money Jarett paid me to cover the deposit.''

"Consider it compensation for all the trouble you went through.''

Meg fingered the stack of bills and frowned. "I suppose.'' But it still didn't feel right to her.

"Rebecca is going to flip when she hears how Harry managed things this time.''

"Oh, no, don't you tell her,'' Meg warned, shaking her finger. "She's already obsessed with this crazy doll.''

"You have to admit, it's all pretty strange, Meg.''

She nodded. "But you're forgetting something—Jarett Miller isn't the man I'm going to marry, is he?''

"You're not married yet,'' Quincy said softly. "And I know you're crazy about the guy, Meg.''

She bit down on the inside of her cheek. "Yeah, I was.''

"Still are?''

"No.'' She shook her head. "It was just a flash in the pan affair. No, I'm going to marry Trey.''

Quincy made a rueful noise. "It's your life and your decision, Meg. And if it's any consolation, I think you're doing the right thing.''

"You do?''

"Yeah. You just don't seem like the kind of

person who would break off a long-term relationship for the love of some guy you've only known a couple of days.''

Meg closed her eyes.

"YOU'RE AWFULLY QUIET this evening," Jarett said over the dinner table a couple of months later. "Do you feel okay?"

Taylor smiled and cut into a chicken breast. "Better than I've felt in years."

At least the trip to Chicago had yielded one positive thing—Taylor had responded well to rehab. He'd been worried she wouldn't take the program seriously because he'd practically blackmailed her into going. But that storytelling stint in the children's hospital had changed Taylor. She'd walked in a starlet, ready to see and be seen. But the machinery and the suffering on those kids' faces had transformed her in a matter of minutes. Jarett wouldn't have believed it if he hadn't witnessed it himself. Taylor had walked out of that hospital a changed woman. She'd breezed through rehab with a positive energy that had surprised everyone, including him. And she'd been clean for the last month that they'd been back in L.A.

More than clean—happy, and definitely more mature. Taking charge of her career, and herself.

Jarett was starting to feel as if she wouldn't even need him around much longer. And strangely enough, where he'd once been sure of what he wanted to do with his freedom if he ever got it, he wasn't so sure anymore.

Meg.

Suddenly Taylor's silverware clattered to her plate. For a second Jarett wondered if he'd spoken Meg's name aloud, something he avoided because it seemed to upset Taylor so much. He'd never known her to be quite so jealous of anyone, although the circumstances had been unusual. "What's wrong?"

"I need to talk to you."

He set down his own utensils. "So talk."

She stood and walked over to a table, then slid open a drawer and removed an envelope. "I received this letter last week, and it's been weighing on my mind."

"Who's it from?"

She turned around. "Meg Valentine."

His stomach bottomed out. "Meg? Why would she be writing to you?"

"She sent me a check for fifteen thousand dollars."

"What?"

"The day of the fire, she thought the store's deposit had gone up in flames."

And he'd paid cash that day—not a small sum.

"So," Taylor continued, "when you offered to pay for the damage, she took enough to cover the repairs and the deposit."

"Twenty thousand—that sounds about right." He'd thought she was pocketing the extra money for her trouble. He hadn't cared—he'd offered more, even.

"Well, apparently, the reason she agreed to be my body double was because she felt guilty about taking the extra money."

"Okay…"

"But the day she left Chicago, she found the deposit—it hadn't burned after all."

"So she's refunding the extra money."

"Basically."

He nodded. "I'm not surprised. Meg is a decent, good-hearted person."

Taylor burst into tears.

Jarett went her side. "What's wrong?"

"I was terrible to her," Taylor said. "She came to the hotel for my help, and I used it against her—against you."

"What are you talking about? When did she need your help?"

"She was approached by a photographer who had followed the two of you, and knew she was filling in for me. He had pictures, and he wanted ten thousand dollars for them and the negatives.''

"What? Why didn't you tell me?"

"Because I thought I could kill two birds with one stone. I told Meg that I'd take care of everything if she stayed away from you."

Jarett stepped back.

"And that if you tried to see her again, she was supposed to ignore you."

He shook his head in disbelief. "You'd do that to me?"

"I'm sorry, Jarett. You know I've always fancied myself in love with you. But now I realize I've been a shrew. I can't imagine why you didn't wash your hands of me long ago."

"Because I made a promise to David, and to your parents, to look out for you."

Taylor sniffed and straightened. "And you've done a wonderful job, but I think it's high time I start looking out for myself, don't you?" She held out the letter. "Go to her. She loves you, I know it. And you've been pining for her ever since we got back."

He took the letter, afraid to give in to the joy building in his chest. Was it possible that Meg did love him? "But she's engaged."

Taylor smiled and wiped her eyes. "Then you'd better go tonight."

20

"AMAZING. LISTEN TO THIS."

Meg looked over the top of her tuna fish sandwich at Kathie, sprawled in her usual chair in the teacher's lounge, reading a celebrity magazine.

"Taylor Gee has just signed one of the most lucrative deals in television. The up-and-coming actress is reportedly going to earn six hundred thousand dollars for each episode of *Many Moons* for the next two years. Gee has enjoyed a surge of popularity since the attack on her at a Chicago hotel a few weeks ago." Kathie lowered the magazine. "Think we'll get that kind of raise this year, ladies?"

Meg smiled, wondering if her girlfriends would believe her if she told them that she had walked in the starlet's shoes, and aside from the man who guarded her back, Taylor's life wasn't all it was cracked up to be. No, she was right where she belonged.

Sharon scoffed. "Forget the raise, I'm just glad

the Gestapo superintendent and the school board has been stopped in their tracks.''

"Right,'' Joanna said from the corner, knitting a new scarf. "Gee, Meg, that was great of Trey's father to go to the governor on the teachers' behalf.''

Kathie clucked. "Especially since you dumped his son.''

Meg smiled sadly. "Our breakup was by mutual agreement. And Trey's father is a just man who didn't mind fighting for what was right.'' Of course, that was after she'd threatened to inform his wife that she was looking spry for someone who had been killed in a gardening accident.

"You really came through for us,'' Kathie said. Then she angled her head. "But I think you need to keep Harry at your place for a while. At least until you're feeling more cheery.''

"Who's Harry?'' Sharon and Joanna asked simultaneously.

"A souvenir Meg brought me back from Chicago—in addition to Taylor Gee's autograph, of course.'' She turned the page and made an appreciative sound. "Wow, Meg, why didn't you bring me the woman's bodyguard instead?'' She turned the magazine around, and there was Jarett, close to Taylor's side. Where *he* belonged.

Meg smiled, trying not to let on that her heart

broke a little more every day. She was sure Jarett hadn't given her a second thought since returning to L.A. The man would live the rest of his life never knowing how deeply she'd fallen for him. "He's incredible, that's for certain."

Sharon looked and groaned in admiration. "Can you imagine spending a night with that man?"

She'd certainly been doing a lot of that lately— in her dreams.

A knock on the door sounded, and Kathie lowered her magazine. "Come in."

Meg took a sip out of her soda can, then noticed her friends' faces. They were dumbstruck— all of them. Meg turned to see what had them so flustered, and she dropped her soda.

"Jarett."

"Meg." He stood in the doorway, dressed in black from head to toe. He looked at her as if he didn't know how she'd react to his appearance.

The bell rang and her friends snapped out of their trance. They slid out of the room, gaping unabashedly.

Meg's heart was going to jump out of her chest. She stood, and the chair clattered to the floor. "What are you doing here?"

"I'm not sure," he said. "All I do know is that I can't *not* be here. Does that make any sense?"

Meg nodded and smiled, unable to talk, afraid to hope.

Jarett walked over to her and picked up her bare left hand. "Does this mean what I think it means?"

"I...gave the ring back to him when I returned from Chicago."

His shoulders fell in relief. Then he walked over to her and took her face in his hands. "I love you, Meg. I know a lot of things happened that you don't understand, but give me a chance to explain. I love you, and all I want to know is if there's a chance you might love me, too."

"Yes," she breathed, then smiled. "There's a chance." Jarett whooped with joy and lifted her in the air, spinning her around. Between her own happy cries, she became aware of another sound—applause? Outside the door of the teachers' lounge, a crowd had gathered and were clapping wildly. Kathie whistled loudly through her fingers.

He grinned up at her. "I didn't just get you in trouble, did I?"

"No," she said, grinning. "Not at all."

"Can you take the rest of the day off?"

"You're in luck," she said, draping her arms around his neck. "My next class is show and tell."

HARLEQUIN® *Blaze*™

presents...

Four erotic interludes that could occur only during...

EXPOSED! by *Julie Elizabeth Leto*
Blaze #4—August 2001
Looking for love in sizzling San Francisco...

BODY HEAT by *Carly Phillips*
Blaze #8—September 2001
Risking it all in decadent New York...

HEAT WAVES by *Janelle Denison*
Blaze #12—October 2001
Finding the ultimate fantasy in fiery Chicago...

L.A. CONFIDENTIAL by *Julie Kenner*
Blaze #16—November 2001
Living the dream in seductive Los Angeles...

SEXY CITY NIGHTS—
Where the heat escalates *after* dark!

And don't miss out on reading about naughty New Orleans
in **ONE WICKED WEEKEND**, a weekly online serial
by Julie Elizabeth Leto, available now at www.eHarlequin.com!

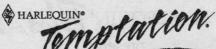

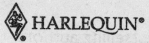